PUFFIN BOOKS

StarGate

As Daniel went through the ring, he saw the silo wall zoom toward him. Before he had time to react, he was out of earth's atmosphere, rocketing through pitch-black space. He glided along for a second; then the StarGate's energy field tossed him head over heels. No gravity, no up or down, only the feeling of his body bouncing off what felt like the walls of a solid steel tunnel.

He passed a cluster that looked like new stars. In the sudden flash of light, he saw his legs stretched out miles in front of him. Suddenly, they stopped moving, and his head whipped past them. He was heading toward a face-first collision with a gigantic planet!

STARGATE™

STARGATE™

From the screenplay and novelization
by Dean Devlin & Roland Emmerich,
adapted by Sheila Black

PUFFIN BOOKS

PUFFIN BOOKS

Published by the Penguin Group
Penguin Books Ltd, 27 Wrights Lane, London W8 5TZ, England
Penguin Books USA Inc., 375 Hudson Street, New York, New York 10014, USA
Penguin Books Australia Ltd, Ringwood, Victoria, Australia
Penguin Books Canada Ltd, 10 Alcorn Avenue, Toronto, Ontario, Canada M4V 3B2
Penguin Books (NZ) Ltd, 182–190 Wairau Road, Auckland 10, New Zealand

Penguin Books Ltd, Registered Offices: Harmondsworth, Middlesex, England

First published in Great Britain in Puffin Books 1995
1 3 5 7 9 10 8 6 4 2

First published in the United States of America by Puffin Books,
a division of Penguin Books USA Inc., 1994

Made and printed in Great Britain by Clays Ltd, St Ives plc

Special thanks to our very own mischievous poltergeist,
Steven Molstad

CONTENTS

1
8000 B.C.

The gazelle scratched on the cave wall with chalk was orange and black. The drawing was crude, but it captured the animal's terror. All the boy had left to paint was the gazelle's eye. When that was done the animal would see him and live. The boy looked up at another eye, a white human eye, painted high on the cave wall.

The boy's own dark skin had been painted with stripes and mystic symbols.

In the cave's murky light, the boy dipped the end of a long hollow stick into a bowl of ink. He spoke the name of the animal, thus marking the beginning of the hunt.

At this signal, the old man standing at the mouth of the cave began to chant slowly. He was leader of the clan and the boy's teacher. His chanting was a hunter's song, spoken in the language of the gazelle. It was the same song the tribe was now singing as it hunted. The boy placed the hollow stick in the empty eye socket of the gazelle. Putting his lips to the stick, he blew out a stream of ink to create the animal's eye. The boy felt the animal come to life. Soon he and the gazelle would see each other.

The boy took a step closer to the cave wall. He dared not move too fast—he might frighten the animal and ruin the hunt that was happening out in the valley. The boy did not feel his own movements, yet under the spell of the old man's chanting, he advanced on the gazelle. The hunters in the field were doing the same.

The best hunters of the tribe were called Those-Who-Walk-Without-Being-Seen. Their symbol was the white human eye that was painted on the cave wall. Even these hunters were amazed by the ten-year-old boy's ability to control the minds of the animals. It was just one more strange thing about this remarkable child, one more reason to fear him.

The boy moved still closer to the painted gazelle. He appeared almost asleep, giving no sign of the mental battle being fought. The animal was on the verge of flight, as it felt the boy draw ever nearer. The boy could feel its every thought, but he showed no sign of emotion. The tribe's hunters spent their whole lives learning to conceal their fear and excitement from the animals they stalked. When they saw that this magic came naturally to the boy, both in the field and in the cave, people said he must have been born without a heart. In fact, the child almost never showed any feelings at all—no anger, no fear, no love.

The old one's chant became slower. The boy inched his thin arms over his head. In one hand, he held a chisel, in the other, a heavy stone. Suddenly, at the same moment, the boy and the old man shouted the name of the animal. "Khet!" Quick as lightning, the boy brought the chisel to the wall and struck it with the heavy stone. When he was done, a deep gash cut across the gazelle's heart.

The old man saw at once that the boy had performed the magic well. The hunt would be successful. Gazing into the boy's strange amber-colored eyes, the old man raised his staff in salute and spoke the boy's name. "Ra!"

That night the tribe feasted on roasted gazelle, and the hunters danced to celebrate their success. They wore eerie wooden masks painted to look like the animals of their world—the jackal, the bull, the hawk, and the gazelle. Only the boy stayed apart from the celebration. He sat far from the fire, watching the dancers. It amused him to see how frightened everyone else was of the animal masks.

At one point, the hunter wearing the jackal mask danced over to the boy. He shook his head and grunted at the child, hoping to give him a good scare. But the boy didn't even flinch. From behind his mask, the man stared into the boy's eyes. A moment later, he stumbled backward in fear. This was not strange. Many of the tribe were frightened by the strange child.

For his part, the boy didn't care what the tribe thought of him. They were like children to him, much slower and simpler than he was. The boy did not know how it would come to pass, but he was sure he would not stay his whole life with the tribe. He knew he could never be part of any group.

While the dancing continued, unnoticed by any member of the tribe a huge triangular shape glided across the sky. It cast a weird, straight-edged shadow over the moon. Sensing an unfamiliar presence, the boy gazed up, but by then the shadow was gone.

Hours later, as the rest of the tribe slept, the boy suddenly sat up. He could feel something hovering over the camp, watching and waiting. A breeze rustled through the camp, then died down again. Soon another gust of wind rose up. This time the wind rapidly grew in strength. Within seconds, it became a gale, waking everyone in the camp. First one tent then another collapsed in the terrible wind. Now the old one was on his feet. His voice rose above the wind, ordering the tribe to retreat to the safety of the cave in the hill.

A light as radiant as the sun appeared in the sky. The people of the tribe scattered in terror. Only the old man and the boy stood their ground. The boy gazed up at the light. He could hear the old one, his teacher, ordering him to safety. His first impulse was to obey the old man, yet his curiosity was stronger than his fear, and the boy found himself walking toward the light instead.

Gazing up at the dazzling white light, for the first time in his life the boy felt an emotion he could neither hide nor control. Overcome with excitement, he lifted his hand toward the light.

2
CAIRO, EGYPT, 1928

The Rolls Royce whizzed past the tumble-down outskirts of Cairo on the highway to Giza. Nine-year-old Catherine Langford sat in the back seat. She had come out from Sweden to join her father, Professor Langford, twelve weeks before. Now they were speeding out into the desert because her father's partner, an American archeologist named A.P. "Ed" Taylor, had sent her father a message that he had found something. "Possibly a tomb," the note said. "Too soon to tell. Get out here at once!" Catherine glanced over sharply at her father. He looked perfectly calm, but she knew he was as excited as she was.

Catherine clutched a heavy book in her lap, *Ancient Egypt*. With her thick glasses and pigtails, she looked like a bookworm, which she was. In her short time in

Egypt, she had done her best to become an expert in hieroglyphs. She had visited the archeological museum in Cairo every day, pestering the staff with hundreds of questions. Now she could hardly wait to see what Professor Taylor had found. Some people were surprised that her proper Swedish father was such good friends with the rough-and-tumble American. But Catherine understood. Both men loved the study of ancient Egypt and were determined to make a major archeological discovery.

Eight years ago the two men had visited the Temple of Ti together. Not far from the Great Pyramids, the Temple of Ti honored the lord Ti, chief astronomer to the pharaohs and overseer of the pyramids. Ti was known as the Lord of Secrets. At the temple, a caretaker had shown the two men a little known collection of papyrus fragments. One of these mentioned that something mysterious had been buried halfway between the Steps Pyramid and the Great Pyramids of Giza. The ancient papyrus said that "a plague, a pestilence, a demon," had been stolen and hidden away there. The clues were few, and both Catherine's father and Professor Taylor knew that their chances of finding the mysterious buried object were small. Yet neither man could resist trying.

Six weeks later, they thought they had found what they were looking for. Near the Steps Pyramid they had discovered a small burial chamber. Archeologists from around the world came to see the find—even the

world-famous archeologist who had discovered King
Tut's tomb. But when the burial chamber was opened,
all that was inside was a mummified cat, still in its crude
wooden coffin. Newspapers around the world made fun
of the great discovery. "The Kitty-Kat Tut," one newspa-
per called it.

Catherine leaned her head against the window and
frowned. Only she knew how hurt and embarrassed her
father had been. Ever since, he'd been working desperately hard to prove that he and Taylor were right, that
there was something important buried out there in the
desert.

The car came to a stop. Professor Langford, showing
his excitement for the first time, bounded out of the car.
Catherine fluttered after him. They were standing on the
edge of a silt-and-stone plateau, thousands of years old.
Here hundreds of Arab laborers had created a small,
shallow valley. It was littered with digging equipment,
and divided into neatly measured parcels by surveyor's
stakes.

Nearly three hundred laborers or *fellahin* were there
that day. Most of them were working around a huge pit
at the far edge of the site. Two giant wooden hoisting
cranes had been moved into place at the edge of this pit.
They were preparing to lift something out of the ground,
something heavy.

"Daddy, the treasure's over there!" cried Catherine in
Swedish. "We'll go see Taylor first," her father replied.

Taylor and a group of other men were bent over a

worktable outside the office tent. They seemed to be studying something. "Hey, Ed," Professor Langford called, as he and Catherine went over to them, "if we've found a pet cemetery I quit." No one laughed at his joke. In fact, no one even looked up. They were too busy staring at the paper in front of them. Catherine peered at it. The paper was covered with strange markings, charcoal rubbings taken from an etched stone surface.

"We can't decipher this writing," Taylor said. "Here, Langford, take a look." Catherine could tell her father understood at once why the group was so puzzled, but she spoke up first. "But those aren't real hieroglyphs," she said in English.

"I know," Taylor agreed. "At least not the kind we're used to."

Her father looked edgy. "Where did these symbols come from?"

"I'll show you." Taylor led her father over to what looked like a giant stone tabletop. It was three feet tall and twenty feet across, and the same gray as the gravel pit it sat in.

"It's a cover stone," Taylor explained, "the largest one I've ever seen. When you bury something under a rock this size, you mean to keep it buried."

A shiver went up Catherine's spine. As soon as she looked at the stone, she knew her father and Taylor had found something truly important. Not only was the stone enormous, but its surface was beautifully carved. On the face of the stone were a series of rings, one inside another like a target. The outer ring contained thirty-nine hieroglyphs written in the unknown style Taylor had shown Catherine and her father. Inside the next ring were symbols that were clearly related to the familiar ancient Egyptian writing. Next was a ring containing arched lines criss-crossing the surface of the stone in all directions. Some of the points where these lines intersected were marked, others were not. Catherine thought it almost looked like some ancient form of geometry. But it was the engraving in the very center of the stone that made her catch her breath.

It was beautiful. Against a background of arching geometric lines was a series of etchings of the Egyptian goddess Nut. Catherine recognized her from her ancient Egypt book. Nut was feeding the Children of the Earth while they sailed beneath her in the Boat of a Million Years. At the center of the stone, inside a classic Egyptian-style carved oval, were six of the strange hieroglyphs from the outermost ring of the stone.

Catherine stared at them. Did the strange hieroglyphs spell the name of some prehistoric pharaoh? she wondered. Or did they spell out some sort of message?

"Very queer," her father murmured beside her. "The inside ring is somewhat legible. This here looks like the symbol for years. 'A thousand years . . . heaven, the stars,' something like that . . . 'lives Ra the sun god.' But I can't make any sense of the rest. Perhaps we've found a new language!"

"If we have," said Taylor, "whose language was it?"

"What are these things over here?" asked Catherine, glancing over at a stack of small, neatly labeled curious objects.

"Those are little pieces of tools and cups and things the workers used when they buried this stone," Taylor explained. "But look at this one." He held up a gleaming gold medallion embossed with the symbol called an *udjat*, a half-bird, half-human eye. He handed the medallion to Catherine. "It was wrapped in cloth and left on the center of the stone."

"At last you've found something lovely," Catherine cried.

"The Eye of Ra," said her father, taking a closer look. "It's very rare to find this symbol on a piece of jewelry. Perhaps it belonged to a priest."

Catherine held the medallion up to the light. How beautiful it was! When her father and Taylor turned away, she unclasped her own necklace and slipped the medallion onto her chain.

"Taylor, if this is a cover stone, what did you find underneath?" she heard her father say.

"We'll both find out soon," Taylor replied. Just then a shout went up from the pit. The *fellahin* were hoisting up the find!

Everyone in the dusty valley knew they were watching a remarkable event: the excavation of one of earth's strangest archeological finds. The *fellahin* pulled the ropes taut, lifting a giant quartz ring from its centuries-long sleep. Fifteen feet tall, and the color of a perfect pearl, the ring was an oversized, beautifully made jewel. Its surface was carved in intricate detail, as complex as a futuristic electronic circuit board, as lovely as a sultan's arm band.

"It's one of the god's bracelets," Catherine cried in awe.

No one present had ever seen anything like it. Although the ring was clearly Egyptian in design, it seemed impossible that ancient Egypt could have produced anything so technically advanced. Seven fist-sized quartz jewels were set into the ring, each surrounded by a golden clasp that was a perfect reproduction of the pharaoh's striped headdress or *Nemes*. Running along the outer edge of the giant ring were the same strange hieroglyphs found on the cover stone.

"What's it made of?" Catherine's father demanded.

Taylor shrugged. "Beats me. The material is semi-translucent as you can see. It's harder than steel, and there's no sign of rust or corrosion. Some type of quartz I suppose, but one I can't identify."

Catherine's father threw his arms in the air. "We did it!" he shouted joyously. He pulled Taylor into a triumphant bear hug. Just then a shout broke out from the pit.

The *fellahin* were all shouting and pointing at the pit. They began to run away from something, abandoning the huge ring before the support poles were in place. It tottered dangerously. Taylor raced toward it.

Catherine's father turned to her. "Don't move from

this spot," he told her, and he took off after Taylor.

Catherine stayed where she was for a few seconds, then ran after him. She stopped at the edge of the pit and peered down. She instantly saw what the problem was. A deep gash had opened up where one of the poles was anchored. Whatever was in the bottom of the gash was panicking all who saw it.

Catherine squinted into the freshly opened hole. "Fossils," she shouted. "Catherine, get back!" She heard the anger in her father's voice, but she couldn't take her eyes off the freakish sight below her.

Half buried in stone, its bones splintered as if crushed by some tremendous force, was a human hand. But next to it was a head that was definitely not human. The head was shaped like that of a giant dog. From its center, a shiny black, almond-shaped eye stared up at her. The chilling head was perfectly preserved. How was that possible? Could it be some sort of statue? Catherine wondered. Or perhaps the *fellahin* were right when they called it by an Arabic word she recognized: *devil.*

Just then Catherine felt herself being lifted high into the air and plunked down again. It was her father. Giving her a stern stare, he ordered one of his assistants to take her away and keep an eye on her.

Catherine watched as the men worked to steady the ring in its upright position. The afternoon light was fading into violet evening. She stared up at the ring, the strange desert jewel, and made herself a promise: No matter how long it took, or how hard it was, she was going to solve the mystery of where the ring had come from. She turned to her guardian. "I'm going back to the car," she announced.

At the car, Catherine hastily thumbed through her copy of *Ancient Egypt*. Soon she found what she was looking for: a picture of the jackal-headed god Anubis, the god who led souls to the Land of the Dead. "Look at this." She passed her father's assistant the open book. "That thing down there under the ring is Anubis! We've got to show this to my father right away!"

3

LOS ANGELES, PRESENT DAY

Soaked from head to toe, toting an over-stuffed book bag, Daniel Jackson trudged north toward Sunset Boulevard. He was a young man, just about to turn thirty. He had blond hair and wore thick glasses. He had forgotten his umbrella and didn't have enough money for the bus.

As he walked through the rain, Daniel shook his head in disgust. Today was supposed to have been the day he was accepted back into the academic community. Instead, it had been the day his career was destroyed once and for all. How could he have known his speech to the world's top archeologists would be such a disaster? Wasn't he the brilliant student who had won all the best scholarships? The youngest person ever to become a professor of archeology? How had he let so much promise slip through his fingers? How had he ended up a broke, lonely, unemployed, and very wet exprofessor?

Daniel Jackson sighed. In spite of himself, he kept playing his disastrous speech over and over again in his mind. He had gone to the conference knowing that many archeologists there thought he was crazy because of the articles on ancient Egypt he had published over the past year. He had expected the audience to be hard on him. But he hadn't expected them to treat him like a total nut case.

Daniel's speech had begun well enough. His old professor, Dr. Ajami, had given him a glowing introduction.

"Here is a young man who got his Masters degree at twenty and speaks eleven languages. I expect his work on ancient Egyptian hieroglyphics will be the standard reference in years to come. Please welcome one of Egyptology's most promising young scholars, Professor Daniel Jackson."

But as Daniel made his way to the podium, he overheard two famous old professors of archeology, Rauchenberg and Tubman, talking about him.

"Another wonder kid," sneered Professor Rauchenberg.

"Yes. I own socks older than him," chuckled Professor Tubman. "But I hear this wonder boy's a little wacky. Seems he thinks the Egyptians didn't build the pyramids."

"Another victim of too many science fiction movies, huh?" snickered Professor Rauchenberg. "Well, at least he won't put the whole room to sleep."

Trying to ignore what he'd heard, Daniel climbed to the podium. He gazed at the ceiling for a moment, then surprised everyone by firing a question at Professor Rauchenberg.

"Sir, what kind of car do you drive?"

"A Ford," the old professor replied, clearly puzzled.

"A Model-T?"

"I'm not that old. I drive an Escort."

"Power steering and power brakes?"

"Don't forget the power windows!" Professor Rauchenberg said, trying to play along.

"I see." Daniel scratched his chin. "So in the unlikely event a volcano erupts in Los Angeles this afternoon, and we're all dug up hundreds of years later by a bunch of young hotshot archeologists, there's really no chance of them mistakenly dating you and your car back to the early part of this century."

"What are you getting at?" piped up Professor Tubman.

"Well, Henry Ford started out almost primitively, with the old Model-A Ford motor car. Then his product slowly developed into the more advanced Ford cars we enjoy today. Which leads to my central question about the ancient Egyptians: Why didn't their culture *develop*? The evidence shows that ancient Egypt's art, science, mathematics, and technology were all there complete from the beginning."

After his audience had had a minute to think this

over, Daniel went on. "What I want to argue here today is that the ancient Egyptians somehow *inherited* these arts and sciences all at once. Then after a short practice period, we see the full flowering of the civilization we call ancient Egypt."

Daniel could hear the audience murmuring restlessly.

"Their writing, for example," he said. "The hieroglyphic system of the first two Egyptian dynasties is very hard to interpret. Most archeologists say this is because it is a crude version of the more complicated writing we find later. But as I have tried to demonstrate in my work, this early written language is already fully developed, with a complex grammar and a large vocabulary. What this means is that the ancient Egyptians were able to move from crude cave paintings to a complete written language in an amazingly short time—in just a few generations."

The audience was growing impatient now, but Daniel ignored them. "Let's take another example," he went on. "The theme of today's conference is Khufu's Pyramid, the greatest of the Great Pyramids of Giza. The same argument applies to Khufu's Pyramid. Most archeologists believe that this masterpiece of engineering must have been the result of generations of practice. According to their theory, the smaller Step Pyramid in Saqquara and the large tombs at Abydos were only warm-ups, leading to the building of the infinitely more complex Khufu's Pyramid.

"I do not agree with that theory. In my view, Khufu's

Pyramid must have come first. The small amount of evidence I have found suggests to me that instead of getting better at building pyramids, the people living along the Nile were slowly forgetting how to build these great structures. In fact, they were getting worse at it with each passing generation."

As the meaning of Daniel Jackson's words finally sank in, a few members of the audience stood up and walked out. Others began to giggle.

"Unfortunately, attempts to determine the construction dates of the pyramids using carbon-14 dating tests haven't given us any clear-cut results. But ask yourselves this question. All the lesser pyramids are heavily carved with the names of the pharaohs who ordered their construction. We usually find painted histories in these tombs praising the godlike qualities of the pharaohs buried there. The pharaohs were the greatest egomaniacs in the history of the world. And yet the greatest pyramid of them all, Khufu's, has no writings whatsoever. Not a mark anywhere, inside or out. Does that make any sense?"

One of the most respected archeologists in the conference, Professor Romney of the university at Berkeley, stood up. "It's an interesting theory, Professor Jackson, one that most of us are familiar with . . ."

Someone in the crowd began humming the *Twilight Zone* theme.

"You're suggesting that Khufu's Pyramid wasn't built for a Pharaoh because there wasn't a name on it, am I right?" Professor Romney demanded. "But what about Vyse's discovery of the quarryman's inscription inside the burial chamber, which had been sealed since construction? It says the name of Khufu plain as day."

Daniel rolled his eyes. "Oh, come on! That discovery was a joke, a big fraud." He knew he should be more polite about it, but he couldn't help himself.

"Before he went to Egypt," Daniel continued, "Vyse bragged that he would make an important discovery. Using his father's money, he hired a team of experts. After several months, they had found nothing. So Vyse fired them all and brought in a gang of miners from his father's South American gold mines. Less than three weeks later, he "discovered" what forty centuries of explorers, grave robbers, and scientists could not find— the secret burial chamber with Khufu's name written in it. The problem is, the name is written in a red ink that appears nowhere else in ancient Egypt and it is misspelled."

"What can you expect from an illiterate quarryman?" Professor Romney demanded.

Daniel did not answer but walked over to a chalkboard. With lightning speed he wrote out a series of hieroglyphs. "These are the symbols Vyse says he found in the secret chamber. Now we all know that Vyse had with him the 1906 edition of Wilkenson's *Dictionary of Hieroglyphs,* where the name of Khufu is misspelled in exactly this way. In later editions the publishers corrected the error to this." Daniel drew an almost identical set of symbols down the chalkboard. "Now isn't that an awfully strange coincidence? In any case, if a quarryman had misspelled the name of the pharoah—especially on his burial chamber—he would have been put to death and the wall would have been torn down and rebuilt."

"Oh, come on! You sound like a bad television show," Professor Romney interrupted Daniel angrily, as he walked out of the room. Some members of the audience cheered, but Daniel could tell that he had sparked other members' interest.

"Now if we could get back to the subject . . ."

"Professor, if I may." An elderly woman wearing thick glasses and a stylish dress stood up at the back of the room. "Your command of the facts is very impressive," she said with a slight Swedish accent. "I have just one question. Who do *you* think built the pyramids?"

"That's the whole point," Daniel told her. "I have no idea who built them, or why."

The woman nodded, turned, and walked out of the room. A groan of disappointment rose from the audience.

"You have no idea who built them?" called a bearded man from the front row. "How about the lost people of Atlantis!"

"Or Martians perhaps!" shouted someone else.

"I didn't say that." Daniel tried to defend himself. But the atmosphere in the room had become like a school cafeteria's during a food fight. Half the audience was gone, and more were leaving. Daniel tried to go on. But it was too late. The last members of his audience were walking out.

Dr. Ajami came up to the podium. "I'm very, very disappointed in you, Daniel," he said. "I thought we agreed you wouldn't discuss this nonsense here today. I tried to do you a favor, but now I'm afraid you've ruined your career. Good-bye."

Wincing at this unpleasant memory, Daniel lifted his head. He was at the door of his apartment building. He checked his mail. An overdue notice from the phone company, and a letter from his landlord saying that he would evict Daniel at once if he didn't pay his rent. Professor Jackson slowly climbed the stairs.

He kept thinking about the old woman at the conference. Why did she have to ruin everything? Why did she have to ask him the one question he didn't want to answer? Daniel stamped down the hall to his apartment. There he met with yet another unpleasant surprise. His front door was wide open.

Burglars! Daniel thought.

Normally, he would have run away, but today he was ready for a fight. Slipping through the door, he picked up the umbrella he'd forgotten and stalked down the hall, waving it in front of him like a weapon.

One of the burglars was going through his desk! Then Daniel saw that it was the old woman from the conference. "Hey!" he shouted. "What are you doing in my apartment?"

The woman ignored the question. She only said calmly, "Now, this is a truly beautiful piece of art." She picked up the statue of an Egyptian woman Daniel kept on his desk. "I'd guess fourteenth century B.C. How did you ever manage to afford it?"

Daniel stared at her. "Please be careful with that," he pleaded. The statue was his only expensive possession, but really it was far more valuable to him than any price it could bring in dollars. "Now what do you want?"

The woman set down the statue, and peered at him through her thick glasses. "I want to offer you a job."

"A job? What kind of job?"

"My name is Catherine Langford," the woman said. "And I have some very early hieroglyphs I'd like you to work on."

"Since when is the military interested in hiero-glyphs?"

Daniel was guessing. He figured she must have shown some sort of official badge to get his suspicious landlord to open his apartment. Also, he happened to notice that the chauffeur sitting in the limousine across the street had a military style crewcut. The look on Catherine's face told him he'd guessed right. "Because, lady, I'm too old to run off and join the army."

Catherine smiled. "I'm very impressed, Professor Jackson. Now I wish I could explain everything to you, but this project is top secret."

"Why should I take a job I know nothing about?"

"Well, you have no friends or family here in the city,"

Catherine replied slowly. "There are bills piled up on your desk. Your landlord told me he just sent you an eviction notice. It looks to me as if you *need* a job. And after your speech this afternoon, I wouldn't wait for the phone to ring."

She peered at him through her thick glasses. "But there's an even better reason you should come to work with me, Daniel."

"What might that be?" he asked.

"To prove your theories are right."

Catherine opened her handbag and gave him a stack of faded photographs. They were pictures of the cover stone her father and Ed Taylor had found in Giza, so many years before. Daniel Jackson's eyes widened as he flipped through the pictures.

"Enough." Catherine snatched back the snapshots and handed Daniel a manilla envelope.

"What's this?"

"Your travel documents. You're going to Denver."

"Denver. Look, I'm not real big on flying—"

"Get over it." She walked out and pulled the door closed behind her.

4
YUMA, ARIZONA

The unmarked car cruised to a stop in front of an ordinary two-bedroom house in the suburbs of Yuma, Arizona. Although it was winter, the noon sun had turned the quiet street into an oven. All the people were inside their air-conditioned houses. Even the dogs, lolling in the shade, were too hot to bark.

The doors of the car clicked open. Two officers from the nearby Marine Corps Air Station stepped out. They were wearing crisp uniforms. It was plain they had come on official business.

The first officer knocked at the door. The other, who was carrying a thick black folder, glanced around. Two bikes were parked in the driveway. A basketball rim hung above the garage door. The house looked as if it had been a happy place once.

The front door opened a crack.

"Mrs. O'Neil?"

The door swung open. Sarah O'Neil, a blonde woman of about forty, eyed the two officers coldly. The expression on her face was angry, yet sad, too.

"Wipe your feet." She turned and went down the hall to the kitchen. The officers walked slowly into the living room. The room was perfectly tidy and decorated entirely in white. Unfortunately, the man they were looking for wasn't there.

"Mrs. O'Neil, is your husband home?" the first officer asked.

The officers could hear her at work in the kitchen. "Yes, he is," she answered.

"Ma'am, do you think we might be able to speak with him?"

"You can try," she called from the kitchen. "Last door at the end of the hall."

The officers walked softly through the spotless room. They passed a mantelpiece covered with framed photographs. One of them was of a family at a pool party: Colonel Jack O'Neil, Sarah O'Neil, and their son, Jack, Jr. The three of them were making goofy faces into the camera. The contrast between the happy photograph and the clean, lifeless room was spooky.

The officers went on. At the end of the hall was an open door that led into what looked like a teenage boy's bedroom. One wall was covered with sports trophies. Sitting in an armchair staring out the window, was the man they had come to see. He was wearing a dirty T-shirt and jeans and had a vacant expression in his eyes. He looked half dead.

The officers exchanged a glance. They could hardly believe this empty-eyed man was the famous Jack O'Neil, one of the most decorated officers in the history of the Marines.

The officer with the folder stepped forward. "Pardon us, Colonel O'Neil. We're from General West's office."

The man in the armchair didn't move.

"We're from General West's office, sir," the soldier repeated.

With a slow, weary nod, the man in the armchair motioned for them to sit down and get on with their business.

Sarah O'Neil walked into the hallway. She could hear her husband talking. ". . . so many years old you aren't even sure if this threat still exists," she heard him say.

"As I told you, sir, everything we know is in this briefing statement."

"Aren't you guys still worried that I'm unstable? Haven't you read my discharge papers?"

"You don't understand, sir," one of the officers replied. "We don't want you for this project in spite of your condition. We want you because of it."

Sarah O'Neil heard her husband take a deep breath. She turned and walked back down the hallway. She had heard enough. Ever since their son, J.J., had died two years before, Sarah O'Neil had dreaded this moment. She was sure the two officers had come to send her husband on some sort of suicide mission. She also knew that the more dangerous the mission was, the more likely Jack O'Neil was to accept it. Jack had never much wanted to live since J.J. had died. Now he would go, and she would never see him again. Sarah walked into the living room and gazed at the photographs on the mantelpiece. She felt as if her heart were about to break.

Twenty minutes later the officers left. Sarah went into the bedroom. Her husband's neatly pressed uniform lay across the bedspread, a sight which brought tears to her eyes. Next to it was the black folder the two officers had delivered.

5
DECODING CREEK MOUNTAIN

Daniel Jackson swerved along a twisting two-lane road high in the Colorado Rockies. The trip, which should have taken thirty-six hours, had taken four days. In fact, Daniel was beginning to think he'd never get there. Then he saw the sign: Creek Mountain, U.S. Government Special Zone. Thankfully he steered his gas-guzzling Dodge Charger off the highway. When he saw the Marines at the gate, he was so relieved he honked and waved.

The Marines were not amused. They reached for their holsters. "Hey, wait! I'm Dr. Jackson," Daniel yelped.

"Can we see some identification?"

Daniel made a violent grab for something on the seat. Before the Marines could draw their weapons for real, he sneezed into it. Then he handed over the papers

Catherine had given him. The Marines studied them carefully. Daniel sneezed again.

"You've got quite a cold there, Dr. Jackson."

"Uh-huh. Allergies. Always happens when I travel."

"Go on!" They waved him up the steep driveway. At the top, he expected to find a military base. Instead, there was only the mouth of a large cave. A dozen Marines were exercising in front of it. Daniel parked and stepped out of the car.

A big soldier jogged up to him. "Daniel Jackson?" The soldier grabbed his hand in a bone-crushing hand-shake. "I'm Lieutenant Colonel Adam Kawalsky. Where've you been? Dr. Langford thought you changed your mind."

"I decided to drive." Daniel never flew. His parents had died in a plane crash when he was thirteen. After that he had never much liked airplanes. "It took longer than I expected." He glanced around. "So this is an army base?"

"I'm not authorized to discuss that."

"Okay. Whatever." Daniel opened the trunk of his car and started to lift out his overstuffed book bag.

"Help you with that?"

"Careful. They're books and they're really"—Kawalsky picked up the bag with one hand—"heavy." Daniel was no wimp, but he couldn't believe how easily Kawalsky carried his bag. The big soldier must be one of the strongest men in the world.

Daniel followed Kawalsky through a pair of huge

concrete doors into a dark cavernous hall. The hall was empty except for a small shack of corrugated tin, with a Marine next to it.

Kawalsky signaled the Marine. The doors of the shack opened. Kawalsky and Daniel walked through them into a small room. Suddenly, the room began to sink. Daniel realized it was an elevator. He watched the numbers flash by. 5, 6, 7 . . . 13, 14, 15 . . . "Uh, exactly what floor are we headed for?"

"That's classified information, sir."

Daniel knew he was joking, but he didn't think it was funny. 21, 22, 23 . . . They finally stopped at 28. The doors opened on what looked like a hospital hallway. Kawalsky led Daniel to an office door. He knocked loudly. "Dr. Meyers, sir?"

The door opened. A balding middle-aged man poked out his head. "Hello. You must be Dr. Jackson. I'm Dr. Fred Meyers, Ph.D. archeology, on loan from Harvard." Dr. Meyers had a stuck-up manner that made it easy to dislike him.

"Where are we?" Daniel wondered aloud.

"A nuclear missile silo," twanged a woman's voice.

Kawalsky wheeled around. "Dr. Shore, until Dr. Jackson gets his security clearance, we are not—"

"Oh, shut up, Kawalsky," the woman drawled in a thick Texas accent. She put out her hand. "Hi, I'm Barbara Shore, the astrophysicist on the team. And to answer you, this place has been converted into a research station. But officially it's still a military installation, so these jarheads act like they own the place." She winked at Kawalsky. "Now, Lieutenant, why don't you show this nice young man to his office."

"Yes, ma'am!" Kawalsky grinned. He led Daniel to a door a few feet away. "Here's where you'll be working."

Daniel couldn't believe it. His office was the size of a warehouse. The twenty-foot-high walls were covered with blown-up photographs of hieroglyphs. There was all the latest computer equipment, hooked up and ready to go. But it was the wall directly across from his desk that caught Daniel's attention. Something huge and round was suspended there, covered with a parachute-sized sheet. Daniel guessed at once that it was the cover stone from the photographs Catherine had shown him. He went over and pulled the sheet to the floor. Then he gaped in amazement.

"Glad you could join us."

Daniel whirled around. Catherine was standing there, smiling at him. "Where did you find this thing?" he gasped.

"The Giza Plateau in 1928." Catherine pointed up at the stone. "As you can see there are two rings of hiero-glyphs. With Dr. Meyer's help we've been able to trans-late the inner ring, which is a very early form of hieroglyphics. But we can't figure out the outer ring. The symbols are unlike any ever found. We've shown them to a number of experts, including some who walked out of your talk," Catherine added meaningfully. "But no one has been able to make sense of them."

Dr. Meyers started on a long-winded explanation of the decoding programs they had used. Daniel listened with only half an ear. He was too busy studying the translation of the inner ring written on a blackboard near the stone. "This is all wrong," he burst out. Moving over to the blackboard, Daniel erased the word *time*, and wrote in *years*.

"I beg your pardon." Dr. Meyers was clearly insulted. But Catherine gestured to him to back off.

Erasing and rewriting with incredible speed, Daniel corrected Meyer's translation, word by word. He was so absorbed in his work, he didn't notice the astounded expressions of his audience. They'd watched Dr. Meyers labor for weeks to translate the message. Now, Daniel was doing it over again in a matter of minutes. They didn't know that Daniel was one of the few people in the world truly fluent in this ancient language.

"There," said Daniel. He moved over to the stone and gave his audience a glyph-by-glyph reading of the ancient message. "Beginning here it says: *A million years into the sky is Ra, sun god. Sealed and buried for all time, his . . .*" Moving back to the blackboard, Daniel erased the last word of Meyer's translation. "Not *door to heaven*. The proper translation is *StarGate*."

"Not bad, for a young hotshot," Dr. Shore murmured.

"And now," Daniel said, "will somebody please tell me why the military has an astrophysicist and an archeologist studying an Egyptian tablet that is five thousand years old?"

"My report says ten thousand."

Colonel Jack O'Neil was standing in the doorway. His uniform was perfectly pressed and his hair was freshly cut. He was completely transformed from the man the two officers had visited in Yuma, Arizona. Even the look in his eyes was now alert and commanding.

Kawalsky snapped to attention. "Sir!"

"At ease!"

Opening his black folder, O'Neil removed a document and handed it to Kawalsky for inspection. "Colonel Jack O'Neil from General West's office. I'll be taking over from this point on. You are no longer in charge of this project." Kawalsky was stunned. So was Catherine Langford.

Meanwhile, Daniel was still pondering Colonel O'Neil's first words. "Ten thousand years!" he exclaimed. "That's impossible. Egyptian civilization didn't even exist until—"

"Actually, the carbon dating tests prove it," piped up Dr. Meyers, seizing the opportunity to tell Dr. Jackson something he didn't know. "Plus the other artifacts found at the site were tested and also date to the same period."

"What about the tomb underneath?" Daniel demanded. "This is a cover stone. There must have been a tomb."

"Not a tomb," murmured Dr. Shore. "But something else. Something a whole lot more interesting than a bunch of bones—"

"Dr. Shore," Colonel O'Neil interrupted sharply, "that information has become classified."

"Oh, come on, Colonel! Dr. Jackson is part of the team." Dr. Shore turned to Catherine. "What's going on here?"

"Here's what's going on," O'Neil answered her. "Effective immediately, no information is to be passed to any nonmilitary personnel without my express written permission."

Daniel knew that nonmilitary personnel definitely meant him. "But I just drove here all the way from Los Angeles! What is it exactly you want me to do?"

"You're a translator, so translate," O'Neil replied. He turned to Kawalsky. "See that all classified information is removed from this office and brought to me immediately. Until then, you are the only person authorized to be in this room!"

O'Neil strode out the door. The others stared after him in stunned silence. Daniel turned to Kawalsky. "You guys can't be serious," he spluttered. "If I'm going have any chance of figuring out what this stone says, I'm going to need all the information I can get!"

Kawalsky didn't like the situation any better than Daniel did. But what could he say? "I'm sorry, Dr. Jackson," he replied stiffly. "Your quarters are directly across the hall. If there's anything you need, just ask. Now I'm going to have to ask you to leave the room."

"Didn't you hear what I just said?" Daniel exploded.

"I have my orders, sir."

"Do you always follow orders? Always?" Daniel shouted.

"As a matter of fact, I do."

"Colonel, wait!" Catherine caught up with O'Neil. "General West promised I'd have complete independence on this project."

"Plans change."

"Maybe, but I'd appreciate an explanation."

"The way I understand it, the folks at headquarters feel things have gotten too loose around here. You just brought in another civilian."

"Jackson was approved!" Catherine protested. She stared at O'Neil. "This doesn't have anything to do with Jackson, does it? What's this about? Why did they really bring you in?"

Colonel O'Neil hesitated before answering. But when he did, Catherine knew he was telling her the truth. "I'm here in case you succeed," he told her.

6
BINGO!

Balancing a tray of hot cafeteria food with both hands, Kawalsky pushed open the door with his boot and stepped inside. As the door closed behind him, he was in trouble. The room was pitch black.

Over the past twelve days, Daniel had made his huge office as much of a disaster area as a messy twelve-year-old's bedroom. Kawalsky knew better than to try stumbling around in the chaos.

"Hey, Jackson, dinner! Turn on the lights, man!"

The lights clicked on. "Good morning, Lieutenant."

"It's almost 8:00 p.m." Kawalsky growled. "Why don't you try cleaning this place up a little?"

"That information is classified."

"Ah, give it a rest, Professor. Here's your dinner. Is there anything else you need?"

"Yeah. Could you pick me up some information? No, seriously, Kawalsky, how about getting me ten minutes alone with the janitor? I'm sure he knows more about what was under this cover stone than I do."

Kawalsky sighed a here-we-go-again sigh. "That might be true, but the janitor has security clearance."

"Look, Lieutenant, you people want me to solve this puzzle for you, right? But you won't give me any information. How about this, Kawalsky. What if someone anonymously slips a copy of a report under my door. They'll never even know I got it! I'll just figure this puzzle out and we can all go home happy."

Kawalsky groaned. "Jackson, come on. Get off my back. You know I'm under orders." Setting Daniel's dinner tray down, Kawalsky headed for the door.

The moment he was gone, Daniel got up. Tonight was the night. They weren't going to lock him in a room with the greatest archeological mystery of all time, then refuse to give him the information he needed to solve it. Grabbing the empty coffeepot off his desk, Daniel headed down the hall. The night guard glanced up at him. "What's up, Doc?"

"How's it hanging, Higgens?" Daniel shuffled toward the water fountain. But once he was around the corner, he raced to Colonel O'Neil's office. Pulling out a fingernail clipper, Daniel jimmied off the cover of the lock. Laying the nail file across it, he short-circuited the electronic locking mechanism—without electrocuting himself—and slipped inside.

O'Neil's office felt about as cozy as the vice principal's office at Daniel's junior high school. There was a standard metal chair and desk, with a computer on top. Against the wall was a row of filing cabinets. Daniel opened them. They were empty. A search of O'Neil's desk also uncovered nothing, just office supplies and a picture of O'Neil's wife and son. Could O'Neil have predicted Daniel's break-in and removed all clues from his office? In desperation, Daniel hit the space bar on the computer, and asked the machine to search "O'Neil Jack." "Please wait" flashed on the screen.

Impatient, Daniel glanced at the wall above O'Neil's desk. Nothing interesting there either. Only a map of the United States, and a chart of the stars in the northern and southern hemispheres. This had to be the most boring office in the world.

Suddenly, Daniel froze. Higgens was just outside. He held his breath as the guard stopped, then continued on toward the bathroom. Daniel figured he had about two minutes until Higgens came back.

The computer screen was now displaying the words: "O'Neil, Jack. Colonel. Retired, two years. Returned to active duty, one month." This was strange. What was important enough about the cover stone to bring O'Neil out of retirement? And why was O'Neil the person for the job? Daniel asked the computer for more information every way he could think of. But the only response was: "Classified. Access denied." At last, Daniel gave up. He was beaten.

He softly opened the office door. The coast was clear. Yet Daniel didn't move. Instead, he glanced back. Wait a minute! What was Colonel O'Neil doing with a chart of the constellations—a star map!? *"A million years into the sky"* Daniel gasped. "Of course!" Not knowing what else to do, he snatched the chart off the wall, then hurried out of the office. He didn't even notice his cof- feepot still sitting on O'Neil's desk.

Chomping on a candy bar, Daniel sat hunched over his computer, working like a six-armed demon. He'd fed O'Neil's star map into the computer scanner. Now he was comparing the constellations with the mysterious hieroglyphs on the cover stone. He began with the con- stellation the ancient Greeks had named Orion, which he chose because it was one of the few constellations visible in both the northern and southern hemispheres. Two of the cover stone's symbols were close, but not close enough. Daniel sighed. He glanced up at his Egyptian statue, which sat on top of the computer.

"Are we on the right track?"

She didn't reply, but Daniel sat bolt upright. He began typing in a new set of instructions, turning the constellations into three-dimensional objects. Now he was getting somewhere. There was definitely a strong likeness between Orion and one of the mysterious sym- bols in the stone's outer ring. The same symbol also appeared in the oval in the center of the stone. But the constellations and the ring's symbol did not match per- fectly. The lesser stars connected to Betelguese to form

Orion's hunter's bow, were missing from the Egyptian symbol. Also, the star Rigel wasn't linked to Sirius in the traditional way.

In the traditional way. How he hated those words. He snapped his fingers. "Of course they aren't connected in the traditional way," he yelped. "The astronomers who made this stone weren't Greek. They were Egyptian!"

Daniel ran to the bookcase. He pulled one of his thick volumes down from the shelf. A moment later, he was gazing at another star map, completely different from the one he'd found in O'Neil's office. He glanced at the computer screen, then at the book, then up into the painted black eyes of his silent Egyptian companion. "Bingo!" he cried.

7
THE SEVENTH SYMBOL

Shortly after dawn on a chilly Rocky Mountain morning, a Cadillac limousine pulled in front of the gaping cave mouth. Inside was General West, one of the most respected and feared commanders in the military. The Marine standing guard at the shack saluted the General and his aides as they entered the small structure. "We've been expecting you, sir."

When the doors opened at the twenty-eighth floor, O'Neil was there.

"Jack O'Neil! How've you been?" General West boomed.

O'Neil shook his hand and lied. "Good."

West nodded. He knew it wasn't true. Ever since O'Neil's troubles began, he'd read every report about O'Neil that had been written. For two years West had

THE SEVENTH SYMBOL

been waiting for the right time to use him again. Now he had the perfect mission. But all the general said was, "Good. Now, I've got a few things to tell you that I couldn't put in the report."

When Daniel stepped into the conference room forty-five minutes later, he got a nasty surprise. He was expecting to explain his new theory to General West alone. But the room was crammed with military personnel and all the members of the team's scientific staff, including Dr. Meyers, Dr. Shore, and Catherine Langford.

This was not good. It reminded him of his disastrous lecture in Los Angeles. What if they all thought his theory about the cover stone was just antiscientific mumbo jumbo? Most of them knew—and he did not—what was buried under the cover stone. Maybe he was just shooting in the dark. All of them were dressed up, too—except for Daniel. He was still wearing his jeans and sweatshirt.

"Dr. Jackson!" Catherine motioned him over. "I want you to meet General West."

"Hi," Daniel said, shaking the general's hand.

"Pleasure to meet you, Professor," West said. "We're all looking forward to hearing what you have to say." His eyes fixed Daniel in an intimidating stare. "All right, everybody," he barked to the crowd. "Let's get down to it and see what this young man has for us."

The room went silent. His heart thumping, Daniel

went up to the front of the room, and stood beside the chalkboard. He felt like an insecure student called up to do an incredibly difficult math problem in front of the whole class.

"Uh, I brought some stuff, some handouts." Daniel passed around photocopies of a photograph of the cover stone. "As you can see, what you're all looking at is a picture of the cover stone. Now . . ." Daniel unfolded the map of the constellations he'd stolen from O'Neil's office two nights earlier. He glanced at the colonel nervously to see what his reaction was. There wasn't any. "Now, this constellation," Daniel pointed at the star map, "is Orion. Although it is drawn slightly differently, it matches this symbol on the cover stone. You see, these symbols aren't fragments of an unknown language. Instead, they are a record of the constellations."

"Excuse me, Professor," broke in Dr. Meyers. "But if the symbol on the cover stone is drawn differently, how can you say it really matches?"

Daniel smiled triumphantly. "Simple," he replied. "The map I've put up shows the Greco-Roman system of organizing the stars into constellations, which is in use today. But the cover stone was made long before the Greeks and Romans, and uses ancient Egyptian astronomy." Daniel picked up the book he'd taken from his shelf. Holding the book open for all to see, he went on, "In this older map, the stars are connected in a simpler way. As you can see, this version of Orion is identical to the symbol on the cover stone!

"Now if I am right, the oval that runs down the middle of the cover stone lists these constellations in a definite order, giving us a precise address."

"An address?" Catherine asked.

"Exactly. Inside the oval is a kind of map. It gives us the seven points needed to chart a course to a specific destination."

"Seven points?" Dr. Meyers asked.

Daniel drew a three-dimensional cube on the board, then marked each side of the cube with a dot. "Uh-huh. To find a destination in any three-dimensional space we need two points in order to determine the height, two points for the width, and two for the depth." Daniel drew a line between the dots on the opposite faces of the cube making three intersecting lines. "The symbols in the oval give us those points of reference."

"You've got six dots there," General West said, "but you said we need seven."

"Yes. These six dots pinpoint a destination," Daniel explained. "But to chart a course, we've got to have a point of origin. A place to start from."

"I hate to bring it up," snickered Dr. Meyers. "But inside the oval there are only six symbols."

Daniel smiled once again. He couldn't believe Dr. Meyers hadn't recognized the seventh symbol. But perhaps the doctor didn't know as much about ancient Egypt as he thought he did. "That's because the seventh symbol isn't inside the oval as you might expect," he replied quietly. "It's down here, just below it." Daniel pointed at the photocopy of the cover stone. There were the faint lines of a hieroglyphic symbol engraved just below the oval.

"This symbol is the point of origin," Daniel said. "It's a picture of the place where the stone was found. This symbol is an ancient hieroglyph for earth. The sun beam shining on the pyramid, here, stands for the god Ra."

The room was silent as everyone stared at the photocopy in Daniel's hand, trying to grasp what he was telling them. Catherine Langford spoke up first.

"He did it!" she cried, banging her fist on the table.

Dr. Meyers frowned. "But there's no symbol like that on the device," he said grouchily.

"Device?" said Daniel. "What device?"

Catherine looked at Colonel O'Neil and then at General West. "You have to show him," she declared. "He's the only one who can identify it for us."

General West looked at O'Neil and nodded. O'Neil nodded at Kawalsky, who flicked a switch on the back wall. The wall slid away, revealing a large window which looked down into a vast chamber below. For the first time, Daniel understood how truly gigantic a nuclear missile silo is. The chamber was as big as a hundred football stadiums.

The floor of the silo was jammed with high-tech equipment. And in the middle of the sea of computers and cables stood the giant quartz ring Catherine Langford and her father had found on the Giza Plateau almost seventy years before.

Daniel stared at the ring in awe. "What is it?"

"It's your StarGate," Catherine replied.

The ring had been mounted on a raised steel platform. It gleamed like a huge mysterious pearl, softly bending the light around it into a rainbow of colors.

"You found this thing in Egypt?"

"Take him downstairs and see if he can identify this 'seventh symbol,' " General West interrupted. O'Neil moved to the door. "Not you, Colonel," West growled. "We have to talk."

Catherine took Daniel down to the silo floor, and then up some stairs to an observation booth. There a video screen showed him a close-up shot of a section of the ring. Now Daniel could truly appreciate the incredibly beautiful and detailed carving on the ring's surface. He could also see one of the seven enormous gold clasps, each of which held a large chunk of sculpted quartz: the seven symbols!

"Even though we didn't know the symbols on the cover stone were constellations," Catherine explained, "we knew they matched the symbols on the StarGate. Our problem was we didn't know about the seventh symbol. Now let's see if you can find it." She spoke into a microphone in front of her. "Okay, let's go."

The inner ring of the StarGate slowly began to spin. His mind in a whirl, Daniel realized the ring had been fitted with some sort of mechanical device to turn it. As he watched in amazement, the quartz symbols moved across the video screen one by one.

"Hold it," Daniel yelled. "There it is." With his felt-tip pen, he drew a symbol right on the monitor. Everyone looking on saw that the symbol in front of them perfectly matched the seventh symbol on the cover stone.

"It's earth!" Catherine exclaimed softly. The elderly woman suddenly looked almost like a young girl. "It's been right here under our noses the whole time. All right," she barked excitedly into the microphone. "Let's run a test."

The entire silo became a bustle of frantic activity. Technicians shouted orders to one another. Dr. Shore took Catherine's place in the control booth and calmly began calling out a series of coordinates, which a technician typed into his keyboard.

The inner ring of the StarGate began to spin again, until the quartz with the constellation Taurus was at the top. Then, with a click, the gold clasp around the stone slid apart until the giant quartz had a clear path to the center of the ring. "Quartz one locked on," The technician proclaimed. The process was repeated for each of the seven giant gems.

Beside Dr. Shore, Daniel silently chanted the names of the constellations as they spun by. "Serpens Caput, Capricornus, Monocerus, Sagittarius, Orion," and finally the point of origin, "earth!"

"Quartz seven is locked on!"

As soon as the seventh symbol was in place, the whole silo began to shake. A strange musical humming filled the air. It sounded like a huge organ, playing first one note, and then another, in a haunting celestial melody.

"What in the world—" Daniel started to say.

"Shhh," Catherine held her finger to her lips. "Listen!"

The strange music grew louder. Then something even stranger began to happen. Seven streams of light came out of the quartz gems, as if someone had turned on a series of giant garden hoses, spouting liquid light. The ropes of light arched toward the center of the StarGate in a beautiful twisting dance.

Before anyone had time to take a breath, the ropes of light gathered and spread, forming a solid, shimmering surface across the empty center of the ring. The light now looked like a thin sheet of mercury. Then, as everyone stared in wonder, it appeared to gain mass. It began sloshing back and forth like water boiling in a cauldron. Suddenly, it exploded outward into the room, sending everyone tumbling backward.

"Turn it off!" someone screamed. But before anyone could do anything, the newly created mass of energy was violently sucked back into the StarGate again, forming a roaring tunnel of light. Then the mass of light, or whatever it was, vanished through the wall of the silo, speeding away like a rocket, roaring into space.

The computers were going wild. "What's going on?" someone shouted. "I don't know," replied a technician. "But whatever that thing is, it's guiding itself, like some kind of missile or asteroid."

Dr. Shore stared at the technician's computer screen, which was tracking the strange mass of energy. "It's traveling clear across space. It's locked onto a point in the Cirrian Galaxy!"

"Cirrian Galaxy?" Daniel demanded. "Isn't that—"

"On the other side of the known universe?" Catherine replied. "Yes, it is."

A phone rang in the booth. Dr. Shore picked it up. "Yes, sir. Yes, right away." She set the phone down. "That was General West," she said. "He wants to send in a probe."

"A probe?" Catherine demanded. Below them a technician was already wheeling out a refrigerator-sized, robotic device: a Mobile Analytical Laboratory Probe. As Daniel watched, the technicians hooked the probe in place in front of the StarGate, which still shimmered with an unearthly light. "Let it go," a technician on the floor shouted. The probe slowly inched through the StarGate. There was a tremendous power surge throughout the building, and an instant later the probe had vanished into thin air.

The soldiers and scientists erupted into cheers.

"What's happening now?" Daniel asked, for the technicians were still glued to their computers.

"They're waiting to see if the probe can send data back through the StarGate," Dr. Shore explained.

A moment later, the computers all began buzzing. Dr. Shore looked at her screen. "We've got it," she whooped. "The probe is in the Cirrian galaxy!"

"Then the StarGate works," said Catherine.

Around the booth complete strangers were hugging each other and exchanging high fives. Dr. Meyers came up. "Congratulations, Dr. Jackson," he said. "You did amazing work."

"Yes," said Catherine. "You're a genius, Daniel." She threw her arms around him.

Daniel looked down at her. He had grown fond of the strange old woman. "Hey, Catherine," he whispered. "You're planning to go through that thing, aren't you?"

"Yes," she replied. "That's what all this is about. When I was only nine years old, I promised myself I'd solve the mystery of the ring. I've been working for that ever since."

The phone in the booth rang again. "Dr. Langford. It's for you."

Catherine took the phone. She listened silently to the person on the other end. Then she said in a grim voice, "I understand, General," and hung up. She turned to the others. "General West says he's very pleased, and we should all be very proud of our good work," she announced. "He also says we're all fired. They'll be taking over from here."

8
MILITARY
INTELLIGENCE

"Is this the army's idea of loyalty?" Daniel cornered Colonel O'Neil at the conference room door. "You pen these people up for months, then just when it gets exciting you fire them?"

O'Neil hardly heard Daniel's words. He was too busy thinking about what General West had just told him. Tomorrow he would lead a team of soldiers through the StarGate. "Thanks for your contribution to the mission, Dr. Jackson," he said. "When there's more to report, we'll be in touch."

"Mission!" Daniel yelped. "When are you going through?"

"All information will be released at the proper time."

"Who's going to make that decision?"

"Military intelligence," O'Neil replied.

"Is there such a thing?" Daniel demanded angrily.

"You've got me." O'Neil started down the hall.

"Do you think you can keep this thing quiet?" Daniel shouted after him. "I'll bet the scientific community will want to know about this."

O'Neil wheeled around. "Who's going to tell them? Everyone on staff has signed an oath to keep this secret, except you. Are you going to tell them, Dr. Jackson?"

Daniel gulped. Something about O'Neil made you feel he could kill you with his eyebrows if he wanted. "I—if I have to, yes."

"Go ahead." O'Neil spat out the words. "But do yourself a favor, first. Pick up the latest copy of the *National Enquirer.* Read the story about the space alien baby with the head of a frog. Then ask yourself if you believe it."

Daniel knew O'Neil was right. If he told the world the U.S. military had an ancient Egyptian space travel device buried in a missile silo in the Colorado Rockies, no one would believe it for a second. Especially coming from him.

"Is there anything else, Professor?"

Daniel swallowed. "Please keep me on the mission," he pleaded. "I've spent my life studying ancient Egypt and—"

"I appreciate that. But the decision has been made."

"I don't care," Daniel raised his voice. "I've dedicated my life to this. What have you dedicated your life to, Colonel?"

O'Neil turned away. "Just pack your bags and get off

this base." His voice was like an ice cube.

"Hold on, Jack, I think we're going to need him." General West was standing in the conference room door. Both of you get back here. I've got something I want you to look at."

Two minutes later, Daniel and O'Neil sat side by side in the darkened conference room. They were staring at a TV screen that flashed images from the probe. The probe's camera panned a huge stone wall, then focused on a glowing quartz ring. Another StarGate!

"Freeze it," commanded General West.

The camera zoomed in on the ring. Daniel leaned forward. "The markings on it—they're different!" he cried.

"That's why I wanted you to take a look," said the General. "The readouts tell us the planet this is on is an atmospheric match to Earth. We're planning a short boy-scout type mission. Nothing fancy. Survey the area inside a quarter-mile perimeter, gather information, and bring it back."

"Your job will be to decipher the signs on that StarGate, and dial everyone back home." The General's eyes met Daniel's. "But here's the thing: I'm not sending my men over there unless I'm sure I can bring them back. Can you do it?"

Daniel took a deep breath. Every fiber of his body was pushing him to say "yes." What an incredible adventure it would be to go through the StarGate and visit the mysterious planet on the other side of the universe. But what about the others? Daniel glanced at O'Neil, and at

Kawalsky, who was running the video machine. How could he put their lives at risk just to satisfy his own burning curiosity?

"Well, can you do it?"

Daniel hesitated. "Yes, I can do it."

"Are you sure?"

"Positive."

"Fine," West nodded. "You're on the team. You leave tomorrow at 0600 hours."

Colonel O'Neil sat in a windowless room deep in the silo. He stared at the huge chunk of rock that had originally been found beneath the StarGate. The human body crushed under the StarGate over ten thousand years ago had become a perfect fossil. Remarkably, the muscled body showed almost no sign of damage. But it was the weird, inhuman skull that drew O'Neil's attention. Ever since he had seen it, he hadn't been able to put it out of his mind. He was sure this was what he would meet on the other side of the StarGate: warriors, at once so advanced and so primitive.

O'Neil knew he had almost no chance of making it back from the mission alive. Even if the others survived, General West had given him secret orders that were almost sure to end in his death. O'Neil didn't care. He felt dead inside already. He just wished he were going on the mission alone.

O'Neil was no stranger to danger. Ever since he joined the Marines, he had taken on the most difficult and dangerous jobs. With his nerves of steel and fearsome strength, he was a natural warrior. Soon he had become part of the most elite company of Marines. His specialty was man-to-man combat. And his work had gradually made him numb inside. More like a machine than a man, people said. Then he met his wife, Sarah.

With Sarah, and their son, J.J., O'Neil had almost felt like a normal person again. He'd been happy. Then J.J. died. O'Neil flinched, unable to bear the memory. He stared blankly at the twisted figure in front of him. Soon he would meet this warrior, and everything would, thankfully, be over for him.

The door clicked open behind him. O'Neil didn't need to turn around to know who it was. He had expected that General West would come looking for him.

"It's cold in here," West said.

"I thought I was doing this mission alone," O'Neil replied.

"You will be," the general promised. "As soon as the team completes their survey and comes back, you'll be on your own."

"I still don't like it," O'Neil said bluntly. "The more people we send through the StarGate, the more chance something'll go wrong. And Jackson could be a problem. He's smart. He won't go along with this, if he figures out what our real plans are."

"Then it's your job to make sure he doesn't."

Daniel had finished his packing, when Catherine walked into the room. "I thought you didn't like to travel," she said.

"I got over it." Daniel liked Catherine and hoped she wasn't upset he was going and she wasn't. "Listen, Catherine—"

"Don't worry," she cut him off. "I'm glad you're going, Daniel. The first time I saw the ring—the StarGate—I knew this would happen. I knew that there would be some incredible journey taken. I just thought I would be the one to take it.

"Anyway, I'll give you a special lead case for your glasses, so they won't be damaged in the journey. If you like, I'll even pack a lunch for you." She smiled to show she was joking.

"Thanks," Daniel said.

"I also want to give you this." Catherine unfastened the medallion she always wore around her neck. "It was found with the StarGate. It's always brought me luck."

Daniel turned over the medallion. "But this is an *udjat*, the Eye of Ra," he exclaimed. "It's extremely rare and valuable. I can't accept this."

"Bring it back to me." Catherine turned to leave.

"Wait," Daniel called. He picked up his ancient statue of the Egyptian woman and pressed it into Catherine's hands. "Here. Take good care of her for me."

Catherine smiled. "I will. Have a good trip."

"Bye!" Daniel sneezed as she walked out the door.

9
DEPARTURE

The team was scheduled to meet at 5:45 A.M. sharp. Kawalsky arrived early and found Daniel sitting in the hallway poring over a book. The floor around him was littered with the books and mess Daniel created wherever he went. "Jackson, where do you think we're going, a library? Get this stuff cleaned up."

Daniel, his eyes puffy with "hodophobia," his term for "travel allergy," just sneezed. Kawalsky looked at him in disgust. "Here, take a Kleenex. Oh, and Catherine told me to give you this." He handed Daniel a manila envelope. Inside was the special case for Daniel's glasses. There was also a note from Catherine. "Here's the lunch I promised you." At the bottom of the envelope were five jumbo candy bars.

Two more soldiers reported outside the door to the

StarGate, Feretti and Brown. Feretti was big and restless, with bushy hair and eyebrows. Brown, on the other hand, was calm and slow-moving. They glanced at Daniel with disbelief, amazed that this sneezing wreck was really coming with them. Daniel ignored them and kept reading. Three more soldiers—Freeman, Reilly, and Porro—arrived.

At 5:44 on the dot, Colonel O'Neil came striding down the hallway. The six Marines snapped to attention, while Daniel slowly shuffled to his feet.

"Does anyone want to say anything before we go?" O'Neil said. He looked as serious as a corpse. Hearing no reply, O'Neil was starting to nod, satisfied, when the silence was broken.

"Achoo!" Everyone in line turned to stare at Daniel, who was wiping his nose with the tissue Kawalsky had given him.

"All right, Let's move out."

The team went down into the silo. The day before, the silo had been crowded with scientists and technicians, but now there were only two men inside. One of them was handling the control booth. He leaned over and said, "Initiating commencement sequence."

Daniel tried to swallow while machines around him whirred to life and the inner ring of the StarGate started spinning. "Taurus, Serpens Caput, Capricornus . . ." Daniel whispered as, one by one, the quartz gems were released from their golden clasps and lined up with the center of the StarGate. Beams of light began to flow into the empty center of the ring. As the seventh symbol was locked into place, the strange humming sound—the music of the quartz crystals—blasted through the silo, shaking everything. The group stepped away from the ring. A moment later, the force field began to thicken and then splashed into the room. It hovered there for a second, defying the laws of physics. Then, once again, it was sucked violently back through the StarGate and out the other side, creating a ghostly tunnel of light.

"Everything is ready," the technician announced into the microphone. "Prepare for final departure."

O'Neil gave a signal. Using a hand-held remote control, Brown, the mission's science officer, sent the equipment cart rolling toward the glowing ring. It evaporated into a speeding shriek of light. Now it was time for the humans to make the trip. A shock wave of fear passed through the group—except for O'Neil, who walked casually up to the mouth of the StarGate. For a moment he stood frozen in midstep, then he vanished like a blazing comet.

Kawalsky ordered the remaining soldiers onto the ramp. One after another, they were swallowed up by the ghostly light. Now only Daniel and Kawalsky were left. Daniel froze.

"Don't hesitate!" Seeing Daniel wasn't moving, Kawalsky jogged up to the ring. He hung there for a split second before he was sucked through.

Daniel inched his way up the ramp, closer and closer to the stormy pool of light. A deep hollow clanging

sound filled the room. It was the sound of the giant concrete doors of the silo closing above him. Like a young
pharaoh sealed inside his pyramid, Daniel was the only
person left inside the huge structure. The technicians
had left when Kawalsky had gone through. General West
wasn't taking any chances of what might come back
through the StarGate. He had ordered the silo sealed as
soon as the team had departed. It was now or never.
Daniel shut his eyes tight and inched forward.

10
THE OTHER SIDE OF THE GATE

Just after his twelfth birthday, Daniel had tried out for his school football team. An hour into the tryouts the coach told him to "run the gauntlet." Daniel stared at the row of bigger boys all waiting to cream him.

"Why would I do a thing like that?" he asked.

"Just do it," the coach ordered. His potential teammates whacked him silly. This convinced Daniel he did not want to be a football player. But it was the only experience of his life that in any way prepared him for his ride through the StarGate.

As Daniel went through the ring, he saw the silo wall zoom toward him. Before he had time to react, he was out of earth's atmosphere, rocketing through pitch-black space. He glided along for a second; then the StarGate's energy field tossed him head over heels. No gravity, no up or down, only the feeling of his body bouncing off what felt like the walls of a solid steel tunnel.

He passed a cluster that looked like new stars. In the sudden flash of light, he saw his legs stretched out miles in front of him. Suddenly, they stopped moving, and his head whipped past them. He was heading toward a face-first collision with a gigantic planet!

Daniel arrived through the other StarGate in pieces. First the toe of his right boot, then his left hand materialized. The top of his nose spread out to become his face. The pieces hung suspended in the light in the StarGate's center for a moment, until more molecules came to fill the gaps.

When Daniel was whole again, the StarGate spat him out and sent him slamming onto a hard floor. He was covered with frost. Later, Daniel decided the frost must be a byproduct of his molecular reconstitution. But at the time, he was too cold and dizzy to think about anything. He felt as if he were freezing to death. He also couldn't breathe. He flailed around, hoping to claw his way back into the StarGate, back to earth and oxygen. Then he felt someone shaking him, "Jackson, you all right?" It was Kawalsky.

The big soldier was sitting up, bleary-eyed. The other team members lay piled on the stairs at the base of the StarGate. Kawalsky pulled Daniel into a sitting position. As the first cool breath of new atmosphere entered his lungs, Daniel gasped and started to cough. "Yeah, I'm okay," he sputtered.

Kawalsky moved on to check the next soldier. Daniel felt the ice crackle on his skin, and began to shudder. The trip hadn't been what he'd expected. He hadn't expected it to be fun, exactly, but he hadn't expected it to be a thousand times worse than the gauntlet, either.

"Everyone all right?" Kawalsky asked.

The others nodded. "Yeah," Feretti said, "that was a blast. Let's do it again." Everyone laughed, even though it hurt. Just then the inner ring of the second StarGate started spinning. Round it went, until, with a sudden click, it shut itself off. The light in its center faded, plunging the room into darkness.

"Okay," O'Neil commanded. "Let's get to work. Start phase one of the mission." The colonel lit a flare, filling the room with a sputtering orange light. The members of the team moved over to the equipment cart.

First, Communications Officer Freeman put together the special video camera the team would use to record what they saw. Next, Brown, the science officer, mounted a miniature radar dish on top of the camera, so they could collect sound and atmospheric data. Meanwhile, Daniel walked over to the nearest wall and examined it carefully. The wall was made of black marble, beautifully cut and polished. Yet there were no markings on it anywhere. Daniel frowned. This was unexpected.

"Hey, Jackson, let's go!" Kawalsky shouted at him. The team had finished putting together their equipment and were ready to move out. At O'Neil's signal, they marched from the StarGate room out into a wide black marble corridor. Freeman filmed their progress.

Suddenly, Daniel grabbed Freeman's arm and pointed. They were standing on a metallic medallion, twelve feet in diameter, which had been carefully set into the floor. A matching medallion was set in the ceiling. The metal they were made of looked like copper, but somehow Daniel was sure it wasn't.

The corridor grew wider. A moment later the men stepped out into a vast hall. It was more magnificent than the inside of the greatest cathedral. Towering, ornamented columns rose up to support its immense stone roof. And the floor under their feet sloped gently upward. To Daniel, the room looked like the great gallery of some sort of temple or monument.

The team's flashlights revealed a steep ramp at the end of the huge chamber. Daniel's excitement was growing now. He had an eerie feeling there was something familiar about this place.

As Feretti reached the top of the steep ramp, he suddenly hit the ground. "Hey, there's a light up ahead!" he hissed.

O'Neil inched up the ramp past Feretti to take a look. A second later, he motioned to the others to follow. Soon they could all see where the light was coming from. The steep ramp led to a smaller chamber. At the end of it was a tall doorway, and beyond it sunlight!

"Conditions are similar to those inside. Atmospheric conditions normal," said Brown, consulting his instruments. Moving cautiously, the team advanced into the sharp daylight.

They were standing on a vast stone pier that stretched out into an endless ocean of sand. Nothing but lifeless brown sand dunes under an intensely blue sky. At the end of the stone platform stood a pair of giant obelisks, half buried in the sand. There was no movement, no sound. No sign of life on this sandy twin of earth.

Only Daniel was excited by what he saw. As he had walked through the giant structure, he had felt more and more as if he knew the place. Now, the sight of the obelisks made him certain. They were exact duplicates of the obelisks found in the ancient Egyptian temples at Luxor and Karnac. The only difference was that these obelisks were not covered in hieroglyphs.

"Hold on," Daniel said to the others. "I want to go and get a better look at where we are." He raced to the edge of the stone platform, past the twin obelisks, and up a sloping sand dune. Then he turned to stare back at where they had come from.

What Daniel saw knocked the breath out of him. It was more than he had hoped for in his wildest dreams. Not only was the immense building before him Egyptian in design, but it was merely an entrance hall to a much larger building, a structure more famous than any other in human history: a *pyramid*. But a pyramid so huge it boggled the mind—at least three times the size of the Great Pyramid of Giza. Yet, unlike that pyramid, this one showed no signs of wear. The smooth quarried stone that covered its surface was all in place, glittering in the bright desert light. And hanging in the sky behind the gargantuan structure were not one, not two, but three suns.

Now Daniel understood why the inside of the building had felt so familiar. It was a far more sophisticated version of Khufu's pyramid. Perhaps this was the very same structure the ancient Egyptians had tried so hard to reproduce. In triumph, Daniel realized that his theories had been right all along. Ancient Egypt had not developed from a lesser to a greater civilization, but exactly the opposite. It had begun as an attempt to imitate a far greater civilization. "I *knew* it," he shouted. "I *knew* it!"

11

A LITTLE WHITE LIE

Daniel sat in the shadow between two dunes, watching Brown collect soil and mineral samples. They were six hundred yards from the pyramid, but it seemed to loom right over them.

Daniel had been back inside the pyramid to search for information—especially hieroglyphs. But the constellations cut into the StarGate were the only markings he could find. The absence of any writing in the pyramid scared and confused him. He frowned, thinking about what the team should do next.

O'Neil was at the top of the dune, looking over the landscape with a pair of binoculars. Kawalsky marched up to him. "Colonel, we've surveyed the quarter-mile perimeter. Nothing to report. It's just a bunch of sand."

"Good work," O'Neil replied. "Let's wrap it up and

move back inside. I want you people back through within the hour. I'll mark the equipment I want left behind."

"Left behind?! Aren't you coming back with us, sir?" O'Neil didn't reply. He only shouted down to the men. "Let's pack it up. Time to head home."

"Head home!?" Daniel grimaced. He knew that was impossible. He gazed across the dunes at the monstrous pyramid.

"Come on, Jackson. We've got to get you back inside so you can get to work on the StarGate."

Daniel gulped. "Sir . . . I need more time. We've got to scout around. There's bound to be other structures here, other signs of civilization. If I can just find—"

"That would be nice, Jackson, but not this trip. You need to get inside and make contact with the StarGate on earth."

"You don't get it. This structure is an exact replica of Khufu's Pyramid!" Daniel said desperately.

The men were all gathered around listening now. "What are you trying to say, exactly?" Kawalsky demanded.

"We're not going to find any hieroglyphs or constellation signs inside this pyramid. No writing of any kind. I checked."

"So?"

"Look," said Daniel, trying to sound encouraging. "The coordinates were marked on the cover stone back on earth, right? So, there must be something like that here. All we have to do is search until we find it."

Kawalsky blew up. *"What?* Your only assignment was to spin that ring and get us home. Can you do it or not?"

Daniel took a deep breath. "No, I can't."

"You told us you could!" Kawalsky roared.

"I thought I would have informa—"

"You thought?" O'Neil's scorn was plain.

Kawalsky grabbed Daniel's shirt, hoisting him into air. "That wasn't the deal, Jackson. Now, listen, you lying little rat, you make that thing work or I'll break your neck!"

"That's enough," O'Neil was ice cool. "We'll set up base camp here. Kawalsky, organize the men to get our supplies."

Kawalsky let go of Daniel. "Why should we set up base camp?" He shouted at O'Neil. "Our only mission was to survey a quarter mile and go on back home."

"Calm down, Lieutenant. You're not in command here."

It was the wrong thing to say. Kawalsky didn't need to be reminded that O'Neil was in charge. He took a threatening step toward O'Neil. But the colonel held his ground. After a moment, Kawalsky backed down. "Okay, men, let's move it! You, too, Jackson." He glared at Daniel.

An hour later the base camp was almost finished. A tent was set up on top of the dune, and the men were hauling the last of the equipment up to it. Daniel was tugging along a large wooden crate. He was sure Kawalsky had given him the heaviest item on the whole equipment cart. Halfway up the dune, he paused, out of breath. He could hear the others talking above him.

"This is just beautiful!" Feretti moaned. "We're stuck here, and that moron will never get us home."

"Quit being so negative," Freeman told him.

"Yeah," said Reilly. "Cool it. If we're not back soon, they'll just turn the gate on from earth."

"Look dimwit," Feretti replied. "Think about how we got here. It wasn't on any two-lane highway. We got blasted through this weird energy cannon at about fifty billion miles an hour. And we were all going in *one direction*. Even if they get the StarGate back there working, it's not going to help us."

"He's right," said Brown. "The beam moves one direction at a time. This is deep trouble we're in."

Daniel felt lower than the lowest rat.

Back inside the StarGate room, O'Neil lifted the last crate down from the equipment cart. Glancing at the door to make sure no one was coming, he took out an oddly shaped tool from his pocket. Then he leaned down over the floor of the equipment cart.

"Base camp is operational, sir!" Suddenly, Kawalsky was at the door.

O'Neil hastily hid the tool under his jacket. "Good."

"I want to apologize for losing my cool out there."

"Apology accepted. Now, Lieutenant, why don't you take this last crate back to base camp."

Kawalsky didn't move. "Sir?"

"What is it now, Kawalsky?" O'Neil didn't bother to hide his impatience.

"Did you mean what you said about not coming back with us? Why don't you tell me what's going on?"

"Just head back to camp, soldier."

Shaking his head in disgust, Kawalsky lifted up the crate and left the room.

O'Neil got back to work. Using the strange tool, he pried up the cart's floorboards, revealing a secret compartment underneath. In it were a pair of large gleaming steel canisters. O'Neil fitted them together with a sharp click. The resulting log-sized device was clearly highly sophisticated. At the bottom of one canister a small metal drawer popped open. A square orange key lay inside it. O'Neil shoved the key in his pocket. Next, he gingerly placed the mechanism back in the secret compartment. Then he went back outside to join his men.

Daniel pulled the crate to the top of the dune and collapsed with a groan. Every muscle in his body ached. He could feel sunburn rising on his face and arms. "Hey," he grunted. "Is there any sun block around here? I'm burning up."

No one even looked in his direction. "Feretti! Porro!" Daniel tried again. "Didn't any of you guys bring sun block?"

"Jackson, we need that crate over here," Feretti said. Daniel tried to lift up the crate one more time As he did, the lid popped open. Daniel jumped backward. Two dozen semiautomatic rifles were strapped inside. "Geez! You guys planning on fighting a war here?" he demanded.

"Well, thanks to you we've got time to fight one," Ferctti snarled. "Why don't you go do something useful, Jackson. Like maybe a little reading." He picked up Daniel's backpack and flung it at him as hard as he could. The backpack bounced off Daniel's chest, sending him tumbling backward over the edge of the dune, and pouring his books out along the way.

Down Daniel slid, books and sand flying every which way. When he finally came to a stop, he looked up to see Feretti grinning down at him nastily. Obviously, getting along with the soldiers was going to take a lot of work. Daniel rose to his feet and started limping slowly back up the dune.

After a couple of steps, Daniel stopped. There, below him, were what looked like hoof prints. They *were* hoof prints. Made by something very heavy, too, judging from how deep they were. Something had been there! Daniel wondered if he should call the others, but they'd probably only laugh at him. He'd better follow the trail on his own. Daniel went down one dune, and started up another. At the top, he glanced around.

That's when he saw it. Less than a stone's throw away was a huge animal. The ugliest, weirdest looking animal

Daniel had ever seen. The creature raised its head and eyed him curiously. About the size of an elephant, it looked like some horrible mixture of a camel, an elephant, and a prehistoric rhinoceros. Its long knobby legs looked much too spindly to support its enormous weight. As Daniel gaped, the bizarre mammal tossed its head and snorted at him.

"Where's Jackson?" asked Kawalsky, when he returned to the camp. All eyes turned to Feretti. "Uh, the professor dropped his books over the side," Feretti mumbled. The men laughed, but Kawalsky wasn't amused. He peered over the side of the dune. Jackson's backpack lay at the bottom, but no Jackson. "I don't believe this! What happened here?" Kawalsky exploded. When Feretti told him, he barked, "Brown, Porro. Get your rifles and come with me. We've got to find him." Just then O'Neil came up. "Porro, you stay," he commanded. "I'll go with the search party."

The weird creature had something bright around its jaw. Something metallic looking. Daniel squinted at it. Could it be . . . it was! The animal had on a harness. Daniel inched closer. Not only a harness, but stirrups and a set of reins.

Earthling Jackson took a deep breath. Here was an unmistakable sign that they were not alone. There was intelligent life on this planet. Creatures capable of making tools and taming animals. Daniel pulled a jumbo candy bar from his pocket. "Here, boy," he said, stepping closer to the hideous beast.

The closer Daniel got, the uglier the animal looked. It had a high humped back and long stringy hair in dirty matted locks. Its face was blistered and oily, and its eyes huge and bulging. As the beast grunted at Daniel, saliva dripped from its gigantic mouth. "Yech!" Daniel forced himself to keep going. The reins and harness made him sure the creature wasn't really dangerous. "Here, buddy, have some candy." He held out the candy bar.

A red X suddenly appeared on the animal's face. A split second later, Daniel realized what it was: a targeting device on a U.S. military rifle! He whirled around to see Kawalsky and the others on a dune behind him.

"Don't shoot!" Daniel threw his arms in the air. "This is a perfectly tame animal. It's wearing a harness." As if to prove his point, the awkward beast got clumsily down on its knees.

"Good boy." Daniel held out the candy again.

"Don't feed it," O'Neil warned him.

It was too late. The creature stretched out its long tongue and gobbled down the candy, wrapper and all. Daniel grinned. "See, perfectly tame." He petted his new furry friend. The animal stank to high heaven! But he seemed to have a sweet personality. "You're a good boy, aren't you? Who do you belong to?" Daniel scratched the brute behind the ears.

Big mistake. Faster than a scared rabbit, the tow-truck-on-legs stumbled to its feet and broke into a headlong run. Daniel tried to step out of its way. But unfortunately his foot was snarled up in the beast's reins. The next thing Daniel knew he was being dragged at top speed across the hot desert sand.

Kawalsky lifted his rifle and fired, but it was too late. The huge animal had vanished between two sand dunes. Kawalsky and the others set off in hot pursuit. Meanwhile, Daniel was being banged along face down in the dunes. Sand poured into his mouth and down his shirt. He wondered how long he could survive this.

At last, the unruly beast trotted to a stop. Daniel, his sand-stuffed shirt making him look like a circus clown, sat up painfully. Amazingly, no bones seemed to be broken. The creature leaned down and started licking him affectionately.

"Get your stinking breath away from me!" Daniel yelped. O'Neil was striding towards him. "Hey!" But O'Neil walked right past him to the edge of nearby stone ledge. So did Brown and Kawalsky. Seeing they weren't going to help him, Daniel got up and went to see what they were gawking at. Then his eyes almost fell out of his head. They were looking down into a deep ravine of white cliffs. And crawling on the faces of these cliffs were thousands and thousands of human beings.

12

SO MUCH FOR COMMUNICATION

Thousands upon thousands of ragged, dirty men were at work mining minerals from the deep ravine. They were organized in groups of two hundred, working on narrow shelves cut into the sides of the steep white cliffs. They were dark-skinned people, dressed in thick robes that covered them from head to toe. Even their heads were wrapped in scarves, in the style of the Bedouins of the Sahara Desert.

Children as young as seven and eight years old worked alongside them. The children's job was to carry sacks of the ore—a white coal-like substance—up out of the valley. They did this by climbing rickety handwoven rope ladders, some of them hundreds of feet long. It was a scene of incredible human misery.

Daniel and the soldiers were astounded. They had

thought they were prepared for anything. But ten-foot-tall aliens with pink heads wouldn't have surprised them half as much as what they had found: human beings like themselves.

Daniel's mind raced. What were human beings doing here, on the other side of the known universe? Could these people be descendants of people from earth? Or were we descended from them?

Just then one of the workers looked up and spotted Daniel. At his cry a hundred heads turned to the top of the dune. In a chain reaction down the busy valley, work stopped as everyone turned to stare up at the small group of strangers.

Kawalsky and Feretti reached for their guns. But O'Neil ordered them to hold their fire.

"Should we fall back then, sir?" asked Kawalsky.

"What would that do?" O'Neil replied. "Since we're here, we might as well meet the neighbors." The colonel started down the slope. After a moment the others followed. Twenty thousand pairs of eyes watched them as they wound their way into the deep ravine. O'Neil was glad to see the crowd still seemed peaceful. He turned to Daniel, who was hanging back. "Jackson, get down here," he shouted. "I want you to try to talk to them."

"What? How am I supposed to—"

"Just figure something out, Jackson."

Daniel cautiously approached one of the miners. "Um . . . hello?"

The man laughed nervously.

"I am Dan-i-el." Daniel gestured to himself. "And you?"

The man looked frightened now.

Daniel tried a formal Japanese-style bow. That was a bit more successful. Several of the miners clumsily bowed back. *"Essalat imana!"* Daniel said then. This meant "Hello!" in ancient Aramaic. The men looked at him blankly. Obviously, it wasn't their language. Daniel decided to try out his ancient Egyptian. It was a language that hadn't been spoken on earth for 1,700 years, which meant no one knew how to pronounce it. Daniel gave it his best shot.

"Neket sennefer ado ni," he announced. "We come in peace!" The miners just stared at him. Daniel tried pronouncing the same words a bunch of different ways, but got no reaction. Either they didn't understand ancient Egyptian or he couldn't speak it. In frustration, Daniel tried "Hello," in every other language he knew: Arabic, Hebrew, Berber, Chadic . . . But nothing worked.

Daniel fiddled with the medallion around his neck, wondering what to try next. Suddenly, one of the miners pointed at the medallion. *"Naturru ya ya! Naturru ya ya!"* he shrieked wildly. He dropped to his knees before Daniel, face in the sand.

In seconds, the cry *"Naturru ya ya!"* was being repeated in every corner of the valley. And all the thousands of miners fell to their knees, bending before Daniel as if he were a god.

"What did you say to them?" O'Neil demanded.

"Nothing. Just hello."

"I said *communicate* with them. Not scare them to death." O'Neil barked. As if to show Daniel what he meant, O'Neil took the hand of a teenage boy in the crowd. "Hello," he said, shaking his hand. "United States of America, Colonel Jack O'Neil."

The boy was terrified. He seized back his hand and raced away through the crowd.

"So much for communication," commented Daniel.

"Hey, look down there!" Kawalsky interrupted. "Someone's coming." A caravan was moving toward them across the valley floor. At its center was an old man in a red silk robe. He was riding on a huge animal like the one that had taken Daniel on his wild ride. However, this animal looked well groomed, and had a richly decorated saddle and harness.

"I guess this is someone important," muttered Brown.

The animal stopped in front of them. The old man in the red robe slowly got down. He walked up to Daniel and fell to his knees, murmuring what sounded like some sort of prayer.

"What's he doing?" Daniel asked.

"We do not know, O Holy Master," replied Kawalsky. Obviously, these people thought Daniel was something he wasn't.

When the old man finished, two young women came up to Daniel carrying pitchers of water and clean towels. They wanted to wash him. "No way!" Daniel protested.

But then his attention was caught by one of the young women. She was beautiful. And strangely, she looked exactly like someone he knew. But how was that possible? The girl wet the towel and washed Daniel's face, then moved on to Kawalsky. Daniel stared after her. He was positive he had seen her before. Then it came to him. The girl was an exact double of the statue he'd left with Catherine. She was the twin of his beautiful Egyptian companion from over 6,000 years ago!

The old man was waving his arms in front of Daniel now, as if to say, "Come this way." Snapping out of his trance, Daniel turned to O'Neil.

"They're inviting us to go somewhere."

"Where?"

"How should I know? Somewhere that way."

O'Neil hesitated.

"Come on," Daniel urged him. "Aren't we looking for signs of civilization? I need information, remember? If we want to find the StarGate symbols and get home, we've got to go with them."

"I think he's right, sir," said Brown. "I've been taking some readings of this stuff they're mining. It's the same quartz the StarGate is made of."

"Okay. Radio base camp and tell 'em where we're going."

The old man led the earthlings out of the valley on a wide curving trail. They were followed by a caravan of miners ten thousand strong.

Daniel walked at the head, beside the old man. He was still trying to communicate. Chattering away, Daniel pestered everyone around him with questions, none of which they understood. The only thing he'd managed to learn so far was that the big ugly animals these people used were called *mastadges*.

As Daniel jabbered on, the old man, whose name was Kasuf, studied him warily. He had been the leader of his people for a long time. The strange visitors seemed peaceful, but Kasuf knew appearances could be deceptive. He wondered silently if these visitors could truly be gods. He hoped they were, for their coming had delayed the quartz shipment, and if they weren't, there was sure to be trouble.

Beside Kasuf walked his son, Skaara, the teenager O'Neil had tried to shake hands with earlier. He was not a miner but head of the shepherd boys who took care of the mastadges. Skaara was also busy studying the visitors, especially Colonel Jack O'Neil. He was angry at himself for having run away from the man earlier, and was determined to be fearless from now on.

As the caravan rose up out of the valley, Daniel kept finding reasons to turn and look behind him. He pretended that he was just scouting out the landscape. But the real reason was the young woman. She was only a few steps behind him. Every time he turned, his eyes met hers. With a sigh, Daniel decided, she was the most gorgeous woman he had ever seen.

Suddenly, something nuzzled Daniel from behind. It

was his friend, the smelly mastadge. The creature was sniffing around for more candy bars. "Get away," Daniel shouted. He tried to shoo the brute away. This made all the shepherd boys laugh, especially one funny-looking short kid with crooked teeth. His name was Nabeh.

"Mastadge!" Nabeh grinned at Daniel wildly.

The caravan had risen out of the ravine and was heading across a long wide valley. In the distance, they could see the high walls of a huge city. In a low voice, O'Neil explained to the men how to enter the city, one at a time: first Brown, then Kawalsky, then Jackson, then him. "As soon as you're inside," O'Neil said, "check for an ambush above and behind. And wherever you are, remember, I'll be ten paces behind you."

The old man, Kasuf, blew a loud trumpet blast on a long animal horn. The tall gates of the city swung open. As soon as he stepped inside, Brown knew that if an ambush were planned, they wouldn't stand a chance. The city's streets were crooked and narrow with tall buildings of sand-colored stone looming up on both sides. There were people everywhere, leaning out of windows, hanging over the roofs, so many people that even the air seemed crowded. Brown walked alongside Daniel as curious onlookers pressed around them.

Daniel was still struggling with his new friend, the mastadge. "No! No!" he was yelping. "Get off me. Don't lick, I said!" At last, he gave up and took a candy bar from his pocket. Tearing off the wrapper, he held it out to the greedy beast. The mastadge happily snatched the bar away. "Not the whole thing!" Daniel protested. "A little bit, I said."

The miners on either side of him repeated his words. "Little Bit!" they cried happily. The foul-smelling mastadge had a new name.

Kasuf led them into a large central square. The buildings there were better made and better kept up than those in the rest of the city. Elaborate geometric designs had been chiseled into their stone walls. Some had carved wood balconies and staircases. There was no sign of any writing of any sort anywhere.

Kasuf stepped up to a small, high platform. As the crowd fell silent, he chanted what sounded like another prayer. Then, raising his staff, he pointed to a huge covered object suspended high between two buildings. At his command, a man on a ladder pulled off the cover.

Daniel cried out in astonishment. The object was a giant disk. The design on it was exactly the same as his medallion from ancient Egypt. As the huge disk was revealed, the city fell to its knees, bowing toward their amazed visitors.

"I think they think we're gods," Daniel stammered.

O'Neil picked up the medallion around Daniel's neck. "Gee, what could have given them that idea?" he said. "What does this symbol mean anyway?"

"It's the sign of Ra, the Egyptian sun god," Daniel explained. "It looks like they worship him. They must think he sent us here."

Just then Brown's radio crackled to life, and they heard Feretti's frantic voice.

The storm came so quickly there was almost no warning. At first, Feretti ordered the men off the top of the dune. But then he realized his mistake. Their only hope was to take shelter inside the pyramid. He got on the radio. "Must abandon base camp!" he shrieked into it. But the roaring around him made it impossible to hear his own voice.

Porro came crashing toward him. "Let's go! We've got to get out of here," he screamed. Feretti nodded, and they started toward the pyramid.

"Come again base camp?" Brown said into his walkie-talkie. "We can't hear you." He turned to O'Neil. "It's no good," he said. "Something's interfering with their signal."

A deep horn blast echoed through the square. Around them people rose from their kneeling positions and began bustling around frantically.

"Something's wrong," O'Neil said. "We've got to head back right now. Let's move." Kawalsky grabbed Daniel's arm. They started across the square. Soon their way was blocked by thousands of hands reaching out to pull them back. Ahead, Daniel could see the city gates. A group of men were pushing them closed.

"Open the door!" O'Neil thundered, racing toward them. The men paid no attention. O'Neil turned to

STARGATE

Kawalsky. "Think we can lift the beam off that gate ourselves?"

"Sure." Kawalsky nodded.

The two of them went marching up to the gate. One
of the men there stepped forward to block O'Neil.
Without missing a beat, the colonel tossed the man
aside. Then he took his pistol from its holster.

"Don't do it!" Daniel shouted.

O'Neil fired three times into the air. The crowd froze.
They had never heard gunfire before, and the sound terrified them.

Still, the same man bravely kept trying to pull O'Neil
back from the gate. *"Sha shay ti yu,"* he said, over and
over, tugging at O'Neil's sleeve.

"Get away from me!" Daniel heard the colonel say.
His tone of voice made Daniel nervous. He was sure
O'Neil was going to start shooting people any second.

As the tension mounted, Skaara, the shepherd boy,
came running out of the crowd. He went up to O'Neil
and looked him in the eye. *"Sha shay ti yu,"* he said
softly, as if speaking to a frightened animal. He pointed
at O'Neil and up at the wall, indicating his eyes with his
fingers.

"He wants you to look over the wall," Daniel said.

"I know what he wants," O'Neil snapped.

O'Neil turned and followed the boy up the ladder.
The two of them were up there for what seemed like a
long time. At last O'Neil leaned over and yelled down at
the others.

"It's a sandstorm. Coming this way."

"A sandstorm," Daniel muttered. "Well, that would have been a great reason to shoot everyone." He glanced into the crowd, *"Sha shay ti yu,* huh?" he said, for he realized that this must be their warning for a sandstorm.

"We'll stay until the storm is over," O'Neil announced.

Feretti, Porro, Freeman, and Reilly fought through the storm. They were afraid it was too late, but they had to try. Lugging their equipment, they staggered up the endless ramp toward the entrance to the pyramid. They felt the sand filling every part of them—their mouths, ears, noses—and stinging their eyes. At last they reached the door.

Once they were inside, Feretti turned on the radio again. "Mayday, Brown! Brown do you read me?"

"You're just wasting the batteries," Freeman told him. "We're not going to get any signal through the storm. We should try again when this thing passes."

Feretti clenched this teeth. "This is bad, man," he said. "This is very, very bad. I was in Saudi Arabia for two years and I never saw anything like this. Not even close."

He wanted to kick himself. If only he hadn't thrown that backpack at Daniel, he wouldn't be sitting here imagining Jackson and the search party suffocated by sand. He also knew that without Daniel their chance of getting home was a big fat zero. He stared at the entrance, where the sand was blowing around like crazy. He wondered if this nightmare would ever end.

While Feretti stared at the entrance to the pyramid, up in the sky above the sandstorm another drama was taking place. The last light of the planet's last sun had faded. The planet's lumpy oblong moon was rising. Suddenly a straight-edged triangular shadow moved across it, blotting out its light. A few seconds later the shadow started a slow descent.

Over the sound of the storm, the soldiers thought they heard something approaching the pyramid entrance. They reached for their rifles. They could hear metal clattering on metal. Then the entire pyramid began to tremble. "Just what we need—an earthquake!" Feretti said.

"It's not an earthquake," Freeman shouted over the rumbling.

Outside, bright beams of light knifed down from the sky as a huge pyramid-shaped spaceship floated into landing position on top of the larger pyramid on the ground. Long mechanical arms unfolded, attaching themselves to the top of the gigantic stone-faced pyramid. This was why this pyramid and others like it had been built. This was the secret of the great Egyptian pyramid of Khufu: It had been built as a landing station for exactly this kind of spaceship.

When the landing was complete, the huge armored walls of the pyramid-shaped spaceship began to move. Like a clever piece of origami, the spaceship's walls

SO MUCH FOR COMMUNICATION

unfolded, changing it into a palace penthouse on top of the larger pyramid.

Now a new presence entered the pyramid. First, a beam of blue light flashed between the two strange metal medallions just outside the pyramid's great hall, the one on the floor and the one on the ceiling. The beam then took on a form. Someone had landed. This new presence stepped away from the metal disks and set off swiftly down the dark corridors.

At the entrance to the pyramid, Feretti and the others held their guns at the ready. They knew something had happened, but what? And what should they do next? Feretti lit a flare, and was about to toss it toward the entrance when he heard something behind him.

He turned to see a jackal-headed creature towering over him. It was too late to do anything but gasp.

13
THE CEREMONY

"I don't think we should eat anything," whispered Kawalsky. In truth, he was starving and wanted to know if the others were going to try the food. "They might take that as an insult," Daniel replied.

The feast was an hour old, but no food had been served yet. The team was sitting with Kasuf and the other city elders at a long table in the central square. There were no women in sight for women were expected to stay in the background. Colorful carpets covered the ground, and torches shone all around. Nearby, a group of musicians plucked at primitive stringed instruments. Then, a long line of serving women dressed in brilliant silk robes came into the square, carrying trays piled high. They set them down on the table, which groaned under the weight.

"Dinner!" Kawalsky happily lifted the lid off the tureen in front of him. "Aghh!" he shrieked. Inside was a giant lizard, cooked whole. Its grinning mouth was pulled back to show a pair of bright yellow gums.

"Permission to barf, sir?" Brown asked, but he was only half-joking.

"They can't seriously expect us to eat this, can they?"

The team glanced down the table. The city elders were enthusiastically motioning for them to dig in. The travelers stared down at their Reptile Special.

Kawalsky grinned at Daniel. "How about a nice juicy drumstick?"

"Hey, it can't be any worse than army food," Daniel shot back.

"But it could be poisonous," said Brown.

"He's right, Kawalsky," O'Neil agreed. "We can't afford to lose Jackson. You taste it first."

Kawalsky was too hungry to be insulted. He picked up a knife and sawed off one of the hideous reptile's hind legs. He took a bite and chewed it very, very slowly. When nothing bad happened, he swallowed. "Not bad. Tastes like chicken."

Kawalsky reached for another lizard drumstick. Daniel and Brown started to dig in, too. Kasuf watched them. He looked as though their satisfaction were a matter of life or death. When Daniel saw how worried Kasuf was, he tried to reassure him. "It's good," he said. "Like chicken. Chic-ken!"

Kasuf gave him a blank stare. Daniel tucked his

thumbs under his armpits and did his best chicken imitation. "Bock, bock, bock."

Kasuf watched him; then he stuck his thumbs under his own armpits. "Bock, bock, bock," he said solemnly.

"Quit while you're behind, Jackson," Kawalsky said.

After that, everyone except O'Neil started to relax and enjoy themselves. Once you got past how the food looked, it didn't taste half bad. Daniel had moved down the table to try and talk to Kasuf using a bizarre mixture of speech and sign language. He was jabbering along when he froze midsentence and gaped. Kasuf looked to see what had captivated his visitor. It was the young woman Daniel had first seen at the mine.

She was even more beautiful than Daniel remembered. Her black hair hung loose down her back, and she was wearing an apricot-colored silk robe. Daniel watched her every move as she slowly made her way down the table, carrying a basket of fruit. She was smiling and laughing at everyone. She was not only breathtakingly beautiful, Daniel decided, but smart and funny as well.

"Here she comes, Romeo." Brown nudged him.

"What are you talking about?"

"You and her. It wouldn't be so bad. You two could honeymoon back at the pyramid. Go dune climbing—"

"Just shut up, will you?" Daniel turned beet red. He shouldn't let Brown's teasing get to him. But when it came to romance, Daniel was a complete dork, and he knew it.

Someone tugged softly at his sleeve. Daniel looked up and turned even redder. She was holding out the basket of fruit, offering him his choice. Daniel felt totally paralyzed. "I . . . uh . . ." he tried to smile at her. She smiled back, then did something that clearly surprised her. She picked up a piece of fruit and gently put it in Daniel's hand.

To Daniel's embarrassment, Kasuf and the other elders began to cheer and applaud. At least, Daniel thought that was what they were doing. The young woman turned and ran away across the square. Daniel stared after her. Meanwhile, Kasuf pointed at Daniel and nodded at a group of older women standing in the shadows.

"Look's like they're talking about you and your girlfriend," said Kawalsky, with a grin.

"Shut up and eat your lizard," Daniel retorted.

"Jackson, come over here a second!" O'Neil was standing at the edge of the square, staring up at the huge disk suspended high overhead. "You said this thing is an Egyptian symbol, right?"

"Uh-huh. It's an *udjat*. Commonly known as the Eye of Ra," Daniel explained, relieved to be talking about something besides the young woman. "There are several different versions of it, but—"

"Yeah, whatever," O'Neil wasn't interested. "The thing is, if these people know one Egyptian symbol, then maybe—"

". . . they know others!" Daniel cried excitedly. "We

can write to one another! Why didn't I think of that?"
He raced over to Kasuf's table. Picking up a stick, he
traced a hieroglyph in the hard-packed earth at the
elder's feet. He wrote the first hieroglyph that came into
his mind: *feast*.

When Daniel looked up, the elders looked as if they
were choking. Kasuf was waving his arms around wildly
as if to say, "Stop!" Maybe that hieroglyph meant something nasty in their language. Daniel tried again: *He who
has come in peace and crossed the heavens is Ra!* It
was the first hieroglyphic sentence he'd ever learned.
Kasuf gasped. Leaping up, he angrily rubbed out
Daniel's sentence with his foot. Then he shouted something, and everyone in the square turned and fled.

"Jackson! Why is it that every time I tell you to communicate with these people, you cause some sort of
explosion? What did you write?" O'Neil glared at him.

"Nothing. They're overreacting. I wrote *feast!*"

"A pretty strong reaction," said Kawalsky.

"I know. It's almost like they're scared of writing."

"More likely, they're not allowed to write," O'Neil
said. "I don't know what these people are so frightened
of, but they're sure scared of something."

Kasuf had come back. Kneeling before them, he
launched into what sounded like long apology. "That's
okay," Daniel was beginning, when Kasuf took hold of
his arm, and started pulling him back across the square
toward a group of old women. The old women were
beckoning Daniel to go with them.

"Should I go?" Daniel asked O'Neil.

"If you want." O'Neil shrugged.

So, Daniel followed the old women through the dark city.

Barely conscious, Feretti was dragged across the marble floor. He felt like he'd been hit by a train. Suddenly, he was slammed down onto a hard surface. He opened his eyes.

He was in a gleaming marble room. In the center of it stood a huge coffin, an ancient Egyptian sarcophagus. Feretti had never seen one before, but as soon as he saw it, he knew that's what it was. Then, the sarcophagus began to move. Its stone walls peeled away piece by piece, like a flower opening to the sun. A long narrow platform came into view. Lying on it was a human body wrapped in a dark wet cloth. As Feretti watched, the body came to life. It sat up and unwrapped the cloth from itself. Feretti began to wail. Before him was a glowing golden face, part human and part something else. The terrified soldier heard something move behind him. A moment later, the butt end of a riflelike weapon smashed into his skull.

Daniel flopped back on the big lumpy bed. He sighed in satisfaction. For the last hour, the old women had lathered, shaved, combed, dressed, and perfumed him. He was now wearing a long white robe, and brocade slippers that could have come out of the *Arabian Nights*.

Daniel looked around. He couldn't decide if this place was an archeologist's dream or nightmare. On the one hand, he had to find a way of cracking the code and getting the team back through the StarGate. On the other, this place was like ancient Egypt come to life, and every detail about it fascinated him.

Suddenly Daniel heard people whispering outside his room. He bolted up, wondering if he were in danger. The curtains parted, and the young woman entered, the beautiful woman he hadn't been able to get out of his mind since he'd set eyes on her. She, too, was wearing a long white robe, and there was a lacy veil over her face. She looked like—Daniel rose to his feet—a bride! And in a flash he realized that's exactly what she was. That was why Kasuf and the old women had been so excited. They were giving Daniel this woman to be his wife. Daniel stared at her, and sneezed.

14

THE DISCOVERY

Daniel stared at the woman, his face as red as a hot pepper. She looked scared. "Hey," he swallowed. "Don't worry, you don't have to go through with this. I mean, I like you. You're really beautiful, but . . . I'm not ready to get married. Understand?" He took her arm and steered her toward the entrance. When he opened the curtains, he got a big shock. Kasuf and about a hundred other people were gathered outside, waiting for the happy couple.

"*Khha shi ma nelay?*" Kasuf barked. The young woman tried to answer, but Kasuf shook his finger at her and started yelling. She began to cry. Daniel looked at her, then at Kasuf and the crowd. Clearly, the woman was going to be in big trouble if he didn't go through with this wedding.

Daniel smiled. "I . . . just wanted to say . . . uhh, thanks for my new wife!" he stammered. "Well, good night now!" Daniel pulled the woman back in the room. She was still crying. "Sorry about that," he told her. "I still don't want to get married. But you can stay here if you want." She wiped away her tears. Daniel looked at her and blushed again. Ever since he'd first laid eyes on her, he'd wanted nothing more than to talk to her alone. Now he had his big chance, and he didn't know what to say.

Meanwhile, in the same building, Kawalsky, Brown, and O'Neil were sitting around the table in the living area of the apartment Kasuf had given them. They were trying to get a signal from Feretti on the shortwave radio.

"It isn't working," Brown said. "Their radio must be dead."

"Keep trying," O'Neil said, fingering the orange key in his pocket. Just then the curtains parted. O'Neil lifted his head.

Their visitor was Skaara, the shepherd boy. All night long, the boy had been following O'Neil around. Now, he ran over and sat right down beside the colonel. "It's okay," said O'Neil in reply to Kawalsky's questioning glance. "The kid can stay."

Ignoring the boy, O'Neil shook a cigarette from the pack on the table and lit it. Eager to imitate everything O'Neil did, Skaara reached for the pack, too. Shaking out a cigarette, he clumsily lit it. He grinned at O'Neil, feeling proud of himself. O'Neil took a deep drag on his cigarette. With a smirk, Skaara also raised the cigarette to his lips. The moment the smoke hit his lungs, the boy's eyes bulged out. He doubled over, coughing and gagging. With a look of disgust, he threw the foul firestick on the floor, never to smoke again.

"Good move," said O'Neil. "These things'll kill you." Then he saw that Skaara was reaching for his pistol. "No!" O'Neil roared, pinning the boy's hand to the table. "No! Dangerous!" As Kawalsky and Brown stared in shock, he slapped Skaara hard. "No, no, no!" The boy wriggled out of his grasp and raced out of the room. O'Neil put his head in his hands.

He was thinking of his son Jack Junior. Even before this, Skaara had reminded him of his son, but now . . . O'Neil shuddered remembering J.J.'s death. Once again, in an instant, he replayed in his mind all the years and hours spent playing with the boy. He had encouraged his son to be curious and daring—fearless, just like his dad. His wife, Sarah, warned him that he was making the boy too reckless. But O'Neil only smirked at her. "You don't understand how it is with boys," he said. Remembering this, O'Neil groaned and banged his head against the table. If only he had listened to Sarah, J.J. might still be alive.

Brown, watching O'Neil's outburst, turned to Kawalsky. "Is it just me," he whispered, "or is something wrong with that guy?"

"Just follow his orders," Kawalsky said. "He must

have been put in charge for a good reason."

"Do you really believe that?"

Kawalsky didn't answer.

Daniel and the young woman stared at each other in silence for an awfully long time. Finally, Daniel said, "I'm Daniel."

"Dan-durr?" she asked.

"No Dan-yur," he pronounced carefully.

"Dan-yur," she repeated. She pointed at herself. "Sha'uri."

"Sha'uri? Okay, Sha'uri. Hi!" Eager not to lose the moment, Daniel kept talking. "Well, Sha'uri, we came from the pyramid. You know, pyramid?" He drew a pyramid shape in the dusty floor. With a gasp, Sha'uri covered her eyes with her veil.

Daniel stared at her. "What is it with you people? I've heard of being afraid of writing, but this is ridiculous. I guess you're not going to let me write to you, huh?"

Sha'uri's eyes met his. She took a deep breath. She was about to take the biggest risk of her life. Kneeling beside his rough drawing, she carefully drew a line across the top of the pyramid. Above that, she drew a circle. It was the same symbol Daniel had found on the cover stone of the other StarGate.

"That's the sign for earth! Do you know this symbol?"

Daniel didn't know it, but Sha'uri had just broken one of her people's sternest laws. O'Neil had guessed right. Writing was forbidden in the city on punishment of death. Sha'uri gazed at Daniel, trying to decide if he could really be trusted. Then she decided that if he really were one of the gods, sent to test them, he would have killed her already. But that gave her another problem. She had to make him understand how dangerous the situation really was.

Hidden beneath a heavy cloak, Daniel followed Sha'uri through the dark, winding streets to a tall stone building with a high, arched doorway. Holding her torch high, Sha'uri led him down a narrow stairway. The stairway stopped at a dead end. But just as Daniel started to wonder what they were doing there, Sha'uri reached into a hidden crevice in the wall. She pulled a lever, and a narrow stone doorway sprang open. Daniel's pulse began to race. He had a feeling he knew where they were going now. Down into the catacombs—the vaults built below a city in ancient times.

They wound down another staircase, much steeper than the first. At the bottom was a square stone cell. Sha'uri raised her torch, and motioned Daniel forward. There, on the wall, showing faintly beneath centuries of dirt and grime, was the same symbol she had drawn for him. The ancient Egyptian symbol for *earth*, which also stood for sun god, Ra.

Astonished, Daniel examined the walls. But the one hieroglyph was the only writing in the room. On a hunch, Daniel began brushing dirt away from the symbol, until he found what he was looking for—another crevice! The hieroglyph was a sign cut into the middle of a secret doorway. With Sha'uri's help, Daniel pushed at the heavy stone door. At last, it swung open. Daniel lifted the torch and looked into the room beyond.

"Oh, my God!" he breathed. He was looking at a narrow hallway five feet tall and fifty feet long. And every inch of its walls was covered with Egyptian hieroglyphs. Daniel truly felt as if he had died and gone to archeologists' heaven.

Sha'uri couldn't believe it either. She had a vague idea of what writing was, even though she couldn't do it. But she had never dreamed that so many written symbols existed. In her world, there were no books, newspapers, or street signs. Her people did have stories, of course, but only spoken ones. If a song or story was forgotten, it was lost forever. Until Sha'uri stepped into the narrow hallway, she had never understood the power of writing.

As Sha'uri looked on in awe, Daniel ran the torch up and down the walls. His excitement grew, for written in panels on the walls was the history of the people of this planet.

The first panel showed a group of the animal-headed gods worshiped in ancient Egypt. Anubis, the jackal-headed god of the dead, was in command. He was ordering Horus, the hawk-headed god, to seize children from their mothers and march them across the desert. The next panel showed some sort of battle between the people and the gods. The gods apparently won, for in the hieroglyphs that followed, they were forcing a huge crowd of people in chains through a StarGate.

The hieroglyphs told of a people moving across the sky, on a journey against their will. Daniel tried speaking the words the hieroglyphs described. *"Nandas yan tu yeewah! Nandas sikma—"*

"Seekma?" Sha'uri asked, the word catching her attention.

"Uh-huh, *sikma*. You know, *children.*" He pointed at the children painted on the panel.

"Seekma!" Sha'uri smiled and nodded.

"That's right!" Daniel yelled. "How did you say that? *Seekma?* Children?" His suspicion had been right all along! Sha'uri and her people spoke a version of ancient Egyptian.

Thrilled, Daniel immediately pointed to another symbol, the word for *god. "Nefer?"* he asked. The hieroglyph was an eye over two feathers. Sha'uri stared at it, wrinkling her brow, but couldn't guess what it meant.

"Ne-far? Nia-fer?" Daniel tried out different ways of pronouncing it. Then, he pointed at a picture of Anubis, the frightening jackal-headed god.

"Ne-youm ifar!" Sha'uri yelped.

"Nay-youm-ee-far?" Daniel repeated. No wonder he hadn't been able to make himself understood. The words were pronounced very differently. But now he was doing it. He was speaking the language of the pharaohs, a language dead on earth for hundreds of years!

"Ne-youm ifar." He grinned. "Now teach me to speak. *Sha'uri takera Daniel.* Okay?"

"Sha'uri tah-ki-yeer Dan-yur," Sha'uri corrected him. It was the first time in her life a man had asked her to teach him anything. Sha'uri swelled with pride.

Brown and O'Neil were fiddling with the shortwave radio. Kawalsky had gone to find Daniel. Brown frowned. "I don't get it. All that's coming back is dead air. Something must have happened."

"Hey," Kawalsky rushed in, holding Daniel's jacket. "Jackson's not in his room, and I can't find him anywhere."

"Well, we've got to find him," O'Neil shot back. "I want us back at that pyramid before daylight." Grabbing Daniel's jacket, O'Neil started down the stairs.

Skaara was sitting at the bottom of the stairs, surrounded by a group of other kids. The shepherd boy still had O'Neil's lighter. The colonel sat down beside him. The other boys backed away, frightened, but Skaara didn't move. "Hey, sorry about hitting you earlier," O'Neil said. "I need your help. I'm looking for Jackson." He held out Daniel's jacket.

When Skaara didn't recognize it, O'Neil imitated Daniel's famous sneezing.

"Ohhh!" Skaara understood at once. Taking Daniel's jacket from O'Neil, he gave the others a command. A moment later, Little Bit, the mastadge that had befriended Daniel, came lurching down the street, led by Nabeh, the short bucktoothed shepherd. Skaara held Daniel's jacket up for Little Bit to sniff. One whiff and the beast was off and running.

Daniel was stopped in front of a panel, staring at it in concentration. It was a cracked, faded painting of a pyramid hovering in the sky. Below it stood a boy king, dressed in full pharaoh costume, raising his arms to the light. The animal-headed gods of Egypt were kneeling down before him.

"*Barei bidi peesh sha'ana?*" Daniel asked Sha'uri.

"*Chan-ada,*" she corrected him gently.

"Looks like you found what you were looking for." O'Neil stooped through the door. Brown and Kawalsky were behind him.

"You scared me!" Daniel croaked. "How did you find us?"

"Military intelligence," O'Neil replied sharply. "I thought you didn't speak their language."

"I didn't. I mean it's ancient Egyptian, but like the rest of their culture it's evolved independent of any—"

"Just give it to me in English, Jackson."

"I just had to learn how to pronounce it."

"Well, what does it say?" O'Neil gestured to the walls.

"Its unbelievable!" Daniel burst out. "These walls tell the whole history of this planet. See, these people came here through the StarGate ten thousand years ago. They were brought here to be workers in quartz mines—like the one we saw!

"See," Daniel stopped for a quick breath, "the story goes that a traveler—*from distant stars*—escaped from a world where his species was dying out. He was searching the galaxies to discover a way to extend his own life. He had amazing powers and knowledge, but with all that, he could not prevent his own death. He was in bad shape, decaying and weak," Daniel paraphrased. "Look here . . ."

Again Daniel rushed over to another series of drawings. As O'Neil listened to Daniel, he became lost in the story.

"It says he came to *a world, rich with life,* where he found *a primitive race, perfect for his needs.* Humans! He realized he could keep a human body alive indefinitely. Once he transferred himself into a human body, he could live forever. That's when he found the boy!"

The drawings showed a crudely etched pyramid hovering over a human form. There seemed to be a bright light. Several other figures were running away. Daniel pointed to the figure beneath the pyramid.

"The stranger came to a village and the villagers ran, frightened as *the night became day.* But one young boy walked towards the light, *curious and without fear.* The stranger took this boy and possessed him. Like some kind of parasite living off a host," Daniel editorialized and continued.

"In this human form, he called himself Ra, the Sun

God, the original Pharaoh, and ruler of all mankind."

"Using the StarGate"—at this, O'Neil became even more interested—"Ra, or *Reayew* as they pronounce it, brought thousands of people here to this planet as workers for the quartz mines. Clearly, this quartzlike mineral is the building block of all his technology, the only way he can sustain eternal life.

"But something happened back on earth, a rebellion or uprising. After hundreds of years of oppression, the people waited until Ra was here, on this side of the gate. Then they revolted, overtaking Ra's guards, and they buried the StarGate so Ra could not return. Fearful that a rebellion could happen on this world too, Ra outlawed reading and writing. He didn't want the people here to know and remember the truth. These drawings here are the only record they have and none of them can read it! It's amazing."

When Daniel was finished, he waited for O'Neil to respond, but he didn't say anything, didn't move. He only stared at the wall.

"Hey," Kawalsky was examining something at the other end of the hallway. "You guys better get over here. Jackson, you've got to take a look at this!"

The big soldier had uncovered a heavy stone tablet almost entirely buried in the dirt of centuries. The moment Daniel saw it, he knew they'd found what they were looking for. It was the counterpart of the stone with map coordinates buried with the StarGate on earth.

"They must have kept this here, hoping one day the

StarGate on earth could be reopened." Daniel breathed deeply, bending over the tablet with his torch. He didn't understand any of the constellation symbols, which was good, because it probably meant they were the constellations as seen from this planet. "If only I had my notebook with me. I wrote down all the signs from the StarGate on the pyramid on it and I could—"

"Your jacket, Sire." Kawalsky shoved Daniel's jacket at him. Daniel took the notebook from the pocket and checked it. "Yes!" he cried. "The symbols match."

"Yeah, maybe, but we've got a big problem." Kawalsky's voice was grim. He moved his flashlight, showing them that the bottom of the tablet was missing. The seventh symbol, the one which would give their point of origin was crumbled into a hundred pieces. There was no way they could fit it together again well enough to read it. Daniel and the soldiers were stunned. How could they get so close, only to have all chance of getting home slip out of their fingers?

"The seventh sign should be this planet right?" O'Neil said at last. "Ask her. Maybe she knows the symbol for this place." Daniel didn't think so, but he asked Sha'uri anyway. She shook her head sadly.

"In that case, we're heading back to the pyramid—now!" O'Neil grabbed the torch out of Daniel's hand. "But wait!" Daniel shouted after him. "We can't go yet. Don't you understand? We can't make the StarGate work without the seventh symbol." O'Neil didn't even turn around.

15

THE GOLDEN SPACESHIP

O'Neil sped out of the city gates. He seemed determined to get back to the pyramid as fast as possible. Daniel had fallen behind. He was hanging back, trying to explain to Sha'uri that he would come back.

"Jackson, hurry up!" Kawalsky shouted.

"Forget him. He's useless to us now," O'Neil said harshly.

Kawalsky couldn't believe his ears. He glanced at Brown. They were both thinking the same thing: The U.S. Marine Corps never leaves its people behind. Even when they're annoying jerks.

Daniel finally tore himself away. "Hey, wait!"

Kawalsky turned. "It looks like we've made some friends, Colonel." Skaara and the shepherd boys were riding after them on Little Bit.

"Jackson," O'Neil barked. "Get rid of those kids."

Daniel made shooing gestures, but Skaara and the others paid no attention. "Colonel, we could get to the pyramid a whole lot faster if they gave us a ride," Kawalsky suggested.

O'Neil acted like he hadn't heard. Instead, he took out his gun, and very deliberately fired three quick shots in the boys' direction. Little Bit took off behind a dune, with the boys clinging to her sides. Everyone stared at O'Neil in horror.

"What are you *doing* shooting at children," Daniel shouted. "What's wrong with you?" Kawalsky and Brown didn't say a word, but it was clear they were wondering the same thing. O'Neil just kept marching. The others had no choice but to follow.

No one turned back to look at the shepherd boys, who were peering at them fearfully over the dunes. Skaara had a crushed look on his face. He couldn't understand why his new idol, Colonel Jack O'Neil, had betrayed him.

With O'Neil ruthlessly counting out the pace, the men were in sight of the pyramid within half an hour. O'Neil squinted up at the huge structure. "What in the—" he exploded.

There were now two pyramids, one perched on top of the other. The golden pyramid on top was clearly hollow because it fit over the other one like a shell. Its gleaming walls had been opened out, revealing the complicated machinery beneath. The team stared at it, wondering what in the world it was.

"It's a spaceship," Daniel blurted out at last. The others looked at him as if he were crazy, but, in fact, he was right. The golden pyramid *was* a spaceship, built using technology so advanced that the earthlings could not begin to imagine it. This was Ra's spaceship, in which he visited his many mining operations on many planets. Ra had not been to this planet in years. But the quartz shipment was late, and Ra wanted to know why.

"I'm sure it is," Daniel went on. "There was a picture of it in that underground cell in the city. It—"

"Can it, Jackson." O'Neil took out his binoculars and stared at the pyramidal spaceship. He shifted the binoculars over to where the base camp had been. He saw only a shred of canvas, blowing from a tent pole.

Now O'Neil was sure something bad had happened to Feretti and the others. He had to make a decision fast. The colonel pulled some flares from his backpack and checked his rifle. "I'm going inside," he announced.

Kawalsky was dumbfounded. Was O'Neil trying to get himself killed. "Sir! Are you sure? Shouldn't we try getting Feretti on the radio first?"

But O'Neil was already gone, moving toward the pyramid like a human rocket. "I guess we should go after him," Kawalsky said.

"I guess." Brown didn't sound enthusiastic.

Kawalsky tossed a rifle to Daniel. "You know how to pull a trigger, Professor?"

"Yeah, but I don't understand what's going on here."

"Welcome to the army, pal."

They caught up with O'Neil at the two obelisks. "Colonel, slow down!" Kawalsky raced up to him. "We want to back you up, but you've got to tell us what's going on!"

"I don't want you in on this," O'Neil replied coldly. Kawalsky caught him by the arm. "Colonel, you're not going in there alone. Just like we're not leaving Jackson behind anywhere. The Marines take care of their own."

O'Neil didn't reply. He was thinking about the device hidden in the bottom of the equipment cart. It was a bomb, strong enough to blow the pyramid to smithereens. A bomb that he had orders to detonate. O'Neil felt the orange key in his pocket. He had hoped to leave his men out in the dunes, sparing their lives. Now it was too late. They were insisting on coming. He couldn't risk telling them what his real mission was. They would have to die along with him.

O'Neil let out a breath. "I've got to go to the StarGate room," he said. "You don't have to come—any of you. I'm going, whether you do or not."

"Two teams?" Kawalsky asked.

"Okay." O'Neil looked at his boots. "Two teams. Jackson, come with me. Kawalsky, you and Brown take the rear." O'Neil leaped up, and took off like a cheetah toward the pyramid entrance. Daniel stared after him.

"Will you move!? Go!" Kawalsky gave Daniel a shove.

Daniel went. But he had to ask himself what he was doing racing headlong into danger with crazy Colonel O'Neil. If he was really so smart, why wasn't he running in the opposite direction? Daniel followed O'Neil into the pyramid's entrance hall.

There, lying on the floor, beside the abandoned radio, was Feretti's helmet. Daniel paused, staring at it, then plunged after O'Neil again. Had he waited a second longer, Daniel would have seen a shadow fall across the helmet.

It was Skaara. Standing on Nabeh's shoulders, he was peering through one of the high, square windows that ran the length of the entrance hall. He watched the soldiers—first O'Neil and Daniel, then Kawalsky and Brown—cautiously advance from pillar to pillar.

O'Neil was flattened against the final pillar, trying to decide the best path to the StarGate room. Daniel was beside him. Suddenly, O'Neil pulled him down. A hulking figure had stepped out of the shadows.

Daniel's eyes almost fell out of his head. It was Horus, the Egyptian god of the sky. It was he who sat beside Ra, judging souls in the land of the dead. Horus looked exactly as the Egyptians had pictured him, with the body of a man, and the huge head of a hawk. Armor gleamed on his shoulders and legs. And in his gloved hand, he carried a polelike weapon. Daniel stayed frozen as the god disappeared into the shadows again.

Farther back, Brown was following Kawalsky when something horribly heavy cracked down on his skull. A second Horus stepped out of the shadows. He struck Brown again with his weapon—a long staff with a strange amethystlike crystal at one end. Brown collapsed, moaning. Skaara, who was watching from the window, gasped softly.

"Brown? Where are you man?" Kawalsky ducked from his hiding place, and started firing blindly. But his rifle was clubbed out of his hands as the Horus warrior bore down on him.

The two of them began to struggle. Kawalsky's strength was legendary in the Marines, and now he used every ounce of it. He kicked the Horus in the stomach, doubling him over, and tore the rifle back from him. But just as Kawalsky was preparing to fire it, a vicious blow felled him from behind. As he lost consciousness, Kawalsky stared up into another pair of flat black hawk eyes. He realized too late that the enemy was working in pairs, too.

Daniel watched, paralyzed. In all the time he had studied ancient Egypt, he had never once thought the gods might be real. "Daniel, I need your help," a voice whispered hoarsely in his ear. It was O'Neil. The colonel pulled the terrified professor back into the shadows. "We're going to the StarGate, and you're going to cover me, understand?"

Daniel nodded.

O'Neil tightened his grip on Daniel's arm. "Okay, listen. Here's how it's going to be. You follow me forward, but keep looking back, understand, and shoot at anything you see. Now, let's move it. Fast." The colonel gave Daniel a shove, and they started running deeper into the pyramid.

What was O'Neil making him do? Daniel asked himself. They weren't even close to the StarGate, and the Horus creatures were probably everywhere. They pounded across the great hall and tore down the long, dark passageway beyond. At last, they stood at the door of the StarGate room. O'Neil checked inside. It was empty.

He dashed to the equipment cart. Daniel followed. "Get back to the door!" O'Neil hissed.

"But, I'm scared! I saw what happened to Kawalsky—" Daniel blathered.

The next thing he knew, O'Neil's gun was in his face. "Get back or you're a dead man." Daniel went back to the door.

Daniel looked at the colonel bent over the equipment cart. "What are you doing? Hurry! Let's get out of here," he pleaded.

O'Neil opened the secret compartment. It was empty. Somehow the canisters had been taken out, without tripping up the special fail-safe detonator. He knew then that they were facing a truly superior enemy. Just then Daniel gave a shriek.

Two Horus warriors were standing in the doorway. And between them was another figure, taller by at least a foot. It was Anubis; the jackal-headed Egyptian god of the dead.

"Put the gun down, Jackson, it's over," O'Neil said.

Anubis prowled toward them, pointing his long, gleaming stafflike weapon at them. Daniel couldn't look at the jackal head without a feeling of horror. It seemed to be at once alive and made of metal. Could it be some sort of helmet made of biomorphic metal? Daniel wondered. Maybe the gods were actually cyborgs. Anubis gazed into Daniel's eyes, then for a much longer time into O'Neil's. At last, he turned and gave a nodded order to the two Horuses.

The Horus guards roughly grabbed the intruders and dragged them out to the metal medallions set in the floor and on the ceiling of the passageway. The guards pushed the captives onto the gleaming disk. Anubis then reached down to his jeweled wristband where he pressed a clear scarab, a gem cut to look like an ancient Egyptian beetle. A needle of blue light shot down from the edge of the medallion on the ceiling, filling the hallway with a ghostly radiance. It proceeded to trace the circumference of the medallions, entrapping Daniel and O'Neil behind a curtain of wavering blue light.

Daniel and O'Neil felt the same freezing burn they had experienced in the StarGate. The next thing they knew, they were standing in a different room, on a medallion of the same design.

This room was completely dark. Daniel blinked, trying

to control his rising panic. A bell clanged out of the darkness. Suddenly there was a rumbling growl and the walls of the room slid open to reveal a sloped row of windows. Golden sunlight came streaming in.

O'Neil and Daniel saw that they were in a vast rectangular room with a high arched ceiling like that of a cathedral. Giant faces stared down from the walls, sculpted into the pillars that supported the ceiling. At the front of the room was a golden throne shimmering with jewels. Above this throne hung a giant gold disk, engraved with the Eye of Ra. It was a larger version of the one Daniel wore around his neck.

A pair of doors behind the throne clicked open. Out stepped a group of children, ranging in age from seven to nineteen. They were dressed in short pleated tunics and heavy gold collars like figures from an ancient Egyptian tomb. They were gathered around a large golden object.

It was a chillingly lifelike statue of the supreme pharaoh, Ra, the god of the sun. The golden statue was a breathtaking piece of work. The god's long arms lay folded across his broad chest. In his hands he held the traditional symbols of his rule: the shepherd's crook, which stood for work; and the whip, which stood for power. His painted eyes seemed to stare at them coolly.

The statue's expressionless face looked a bit like the famous golden death mask of Tutankhamen, but it was a thousand times more lifelike. Daniel was wishing he could move closer and examine the statue more fully, when suddenly it moved. It was alive! Slowly and deliberately, the golden creature stepped forward and sat down on its gleaming throne.

"Pharaoh King Ra!" Daniel whispered somewhere between terror and delight. Ra's golden skin seemed to glow, giving off a ghostly light. Just like the StarGate, Daniel thought.

Ra stared at his prisoners, then slowly lifted a hand and flicked his finger toward Anubis. At his master's command, the jackal-headed god touched a jewel at his throat. All at once, his jackal head began to melt away, beginning at the snout. The terrifying helmet was made of some kind of "smart metal"—a substance capable of remembering and carrying out a complicated series of commands. The headpiece vanished section by section, revealing a human face beneath.

It was the face of a strong, handsome young man. The helmet was now only a jeweled collar around his thick neck. O'Neil and Jackson watched in amazement and fear. They had never seen technology this advanced. Ra smiled and nodded at the children around him. The children parted, and out stepped a boy and girl no more than ten years old. They were carrying a large silver tray. On it was the device O'Neil had expected to find in the secret compartment in the equipment cart. It had been completely taken apart.

The children set the tray at the prisoners' feet. Daniel stared at it. "What is that thing?" Daniel whispered out of the side of his mouth. "It's a bomb, isn't it?"

At first, he was angry. A bomb? How could O'Neil do such a violent, stupid thing? But his anger was overtaken by a cold stab of fear. He was sure that he and O'Neil were about to die.

Daniel looked up at Ra. The golden pharaoh was leaning forward in his throne. He was changing. His skin was slowly losing its golden sheen. Bit by bit, his pharaoh's mask was folding away from his face. Beneath it was the proud, handsome face of Ra, the boy-king. He looked only about twenty years old, his face untouched by time.

The guards, who considered this boy-king their god, turned their eyes to the floor. O'Neil, seeing his chance, sprang into attack. He rammed into Anubis, seizing his weapon, and knocking him to the ground. He then touched the lever on the god's staff, turning the weapon's laser beam on the first Horus guard, who fell shrieking to the floor.

At the first sign of trouble, the children had formed a human shield around Ra. O'Neil pointed the weapon at them. He knew he should shoot, but he couldn't bring himself to fire on unarmed children. Instead, he turned the weapon on the second Horus guard. But the guard had already drawn his weapon. Daniel, who was watching in horror, jumped forward to warn O'Neil just as the Horus fired.

The shot ripped through Daniel's chest. He felt the room swim around him and knew he was dying. O'Neil, meanwhile, blasted away at the guard, who fell down dead, too. He then stopped to examine Daniel. A mistake. Anubis had replaced his helmet, and he rose up and fired a laser at O'Neil from behind. The colonel tumbled to the floor.

Anubis bent over O'Neil to see if he was still breathing. Discovering that he was, he dragged him out of the throne room by his collar.

Now Ra, still surrounded by his child slaves, came across the floor toward Daniel's body. He noticed that the shot had torn right through the prisoner's heart, which made him smile. Then he noticed something that made him very angry. He picked up the medallion around Daniel's neck and stared at it. It was an *udjat*, the sacred Eye of Ra.

16

THE WRATH OF RA

Feretti was wearing out the metal on his belt buckle. He'd been trying for an hour to scratch the hard stone wall of the cell. He wanted to leave a sign to anyone unlucky enough to get thrown in there after he was gone.

The thick bars across the ceiling—the only way in or out—slid open. O'Neil came tumbling down. His unconscious body hit bottom with a splash. The cell was filled with just enough water to make it impossible to lie down. Prisoners had to squat or stand.

The cold water woke the colonel up right away. He came up swinging, until a pair of strong arms locked around him.

"Sir, it's me, Kawalsky! Are you all right?"

O'Neil stopped fighting and looked around, his eyes

getting used to the darkness of the cell. Brown's body lay facedown in the water. Porro was floating nearby. He was dead as well.

"What happened to them?" he asked, but no one answered.

"What happened to Jackson?" Feretti and Freeman both asked. O'Neil sat down. "Jackson's dead," he said.

At the top of the dune, Little Bit howled at the noonday suns. The shepherd boys looked to see if anyone was coming. When they saw no one, they yelled at the mangy beast to keep quiet, then returned to their treasure hunt. The boys had discovered the soldiers' abandoned base camp. Now they were digging as much equipment as they could out of the sand. They had already dug up the box of rifles. Nabeh uncovered a strange green bowl with a leather strap dangling from its brim. He was puzzled, until Skaara set it on his head. His crooked teeth poking out of his mouth, Nabeh beamed, delighted with his new headpiece.

A loud sound came from the pyramid. A door opened in pyramid's side. Out of it rocketed two one-man gliders, or *udajeets,* followed by a larger aircraft. Rabhi and Aksah, two other boys, sprang over the side of the dune. But Nabeh stayed where he was, like a deer caught in headlights. Skaara ran back and dragged his friend to safety.

There was no time to dig themselves under the sand before the udajeets passed overhead. But the pilots did not spot them. Skaara sighed with relief before he saw that the udajeets were heading toward the city, Nagada. He knew this meant trouble.

The shepherd boys hastily loaded up Little Bit with the equipment from the base camp, and set off. As they drew in sight of the city, they saw a great cloud of smoke. Ra's soldiers had rained fire and destruction down on Nagada. As they neared the city gates, a glider swooped down over the boys. The Horus guard inside it examined them carefully, flying on only when he was sure the children were just returning from the mining pit.

Hearts pounding, the boys led Little Bit through the city gates. The destruction inside was even more terrible than they had feared. Flames and smoke choked the air, and the streets were full of dead and wounded people. Rabhi and Aksah rushed Little Bit to the stables. Meanwhile, Skaara and Nabeh continued on into the central square.

There the situation was even worse. There were dead people everywhere. Skaara felt as if it was the end of the world. Then he spotted his half sister, Sha'uri. She had been cut on the side of the face and was covered in blood, but she was busy organizing the survivors to help the wounded. Skaara stared at her in admiration. He never would have guessed that his half sister could be so strong. But then, her voice cracking, she asked. "Where is Dan-yer?"

Skaara didn't know how to answer. He had watched

as the soldiers were attacked by the Horus guards, but he did not know the fate of either Daniel or O'Neil. He turned away, pretending he hadn't heard Sha'uri's question. As he did, he saw something that made his sadness even stronger. People were pointing up at the huge metallic disk across the square. There, bound to the disk's gleaming surface, was his father, Kasuf, leader of Nagada. Ra's messengers had beaten him and hung him up there.

Tears in his eyes, Skaara demanded, "Why? Why, did this happen to us? We didn't do anything wrong."

"It's the visitors. They are false gods," replied an old man. "They tricked us into praising them, and angered the almighty Ra."

"No, that is not true!" Skaara tried to argue.

"Yes, it is," said the old man. "Now we must repent and serve Ra obediently."

Skaara turned away in anger and confusion. Could what the old man was saying be true? If it was, then, he, too, had helped harm his own people. Skaara gazed across the square. If only he could get Kasuf down safely, perhaps his wise old father could explain everything to him.

Skaara turned and raced to the stables. He fetched a long length of rope, a harness, and a heavy shoe.

When he returned to the central square, he saw that a piece of canvas had been stretched out below the medallion forming a safety net to catch Kasuf. All that remained was for someone to somehow cut him down.

Skaara shimmied up to the roof of the building from which the medallion was suspended. The harness in one hand, the rope and shoe in the other, he tightrope walked along the thickest rope supporting the medallion. Kasuf's eyes widened as he saw his son approaching. "Are you all right?" Skaara asked.

"Shame is worse than death," replied Kasuf. He turned his eyes away, but not so quickly that Skaara couldn't see that they were filled with tears.

Skaara swallowed. He couldn't believe this broken man was his own father, their wise leader. "I'm going to tie this harness around you, Father, so keep still," he said softly.

First, Skaara anchored his leg between the thick rope and the disk. Next he flipped himself off the rope, so he was hanging upside down, chin to chin with Kasuf. Skaara had never worked upside down before, but he was an expert at getting a harness on any creature—man or beast. Soon the harness was tied tightly around Kasuf's middle, and the long length of rope was fastened to it. Skaara tied the shoe around the end of the rope, and tossed it over the thick rope above, and down to the waiting crowd below, where it was caught. "All right, I'm going to cut him loose," he called.

Skaara took a knife from his pocket, and cut the ropes binding his father to the medallion. Now the only thing holding Kasuf in the air was Skaara's harness and rope. As the crowd gradually released the rope attached to the harness, Kasuf slowly spun down. Then the rope slithered loose, and the old man tumbled into the safety net. A cheer rose from the crowd.

One of the men tossed the harness rope back up to Skaara, who hastily tied it around himself, and told them to bring him down. But when Skaara was about thirty feet off the ground, he surprised the crowd again. "Catch me!" he shouted. He untied the harness and plunged toward the safety net, certain that Sha'uri, Nabeh, and the others would indeed catch him.

17

ONLY ONE RA

Silent and still, the sarcophagus sat in the center of the room. Then the sides of the ancient coffin began to pull away. Inside lay a motionless human figure covered with a velvet cloth, a death shroud. A minute later, a spasm racked the body on the slab, leaving it gasping for air. It sat up and tore away the cloth.

It was Daniel, reborn. It took several minutes for him to begin breathing normally. His lungs seemed to have forgotten their job. Daniel dizzily sat up, and was startled to notice a small boy beside him.

The boy beckoned to Daniel to follow him. Daniel hesitated, then slid down from the slab. The boy led him through the throne room to another room. Here clouds of steam billowed up, sending white silk curtains waving to and fro.

Daniel peered into the steam. Although he'd lost his glasses, he could see perfectly. He felt stronger, too. His sleep—or whatever it was—had done him good. He was standing at the edge of a round shallow pool. In the center, sitting in water up to his shoulders, was Ra.

Ra stared at Daniel with his cold, amber eyes. He snapped his fingers for his robe, and lightly stepped out of the steaming water. His skin was no longer gold, but a burned almond color. Nevertheless, Daniel thought, there was no mistaking Ra for an ordinary mortal. If the story in the catacomb was true, the youth before him was at least ten thousand years old.

"I died!" Daniel spoke in the language Sha'uri had taught him.

Ra stepped into the robe held by outstretched children's hands. When he heard Daniel's mispronounced words, he almost smiled.

"That is why I chose your race. Your bodies are so easily repaired." Ra turned and walked out of the room.

Daniel and the children followed as Ra led them down the length of the throne room, up the stairs, and past the throne itself into his private chamber.

The room was cluttered with fantastic works of art, beautiful furniture, and trinkets of all sizes. On a long marble table, arranged like a museum display, were the team's captured belongings: rifles, pistols, field radios, spare ammunition, and Daniel's books. One of them lay open as if someone had been studying. At the end of the table was the disassembled bomb.

Ra spoke to Daniel in a voice which was velvet and croaking at the same time.

"Your people have advanced much since I left," the boy-king said. "Your world has become dangerous." His dialect seemed slightly different from Sha'uri's. Daniel didn't understand every word, but he gathered Ra's meaning.

"You have harnessed the power of the atom," Ra said, gesturing towards the dismantled nuclear bomb. "But you still do not fully understand my power. The power within the quartz mineral."

"What do you plan to do?" Daniel asked, understanding that Ra was boasting.

"You should not have reopened the gateway," he rasped. "Soon, I will send your weapon back to your world. I will pack it in a shipment of this planet's precious mineral. That will increase your weapon's destructive power a hundred times." A smile crossed his lips.

"Why would you do such a thing?" Daniel asked.

"Why? I created your culture, your language, your arts, your government. I created your entire civilization," declared Ra, who moved uncomfortably close to Daniel. "And now, I will destroy it."

The blood drained out of Daniel's face. His dread seemed to please Ra.

"Why did you give me back my life?" Daniel wondered if there was still a way out.

"Because I need you. You will restore the faith of these people in the power of their one supreme god."

"Faith?" Daniel was confused.

"An early discovery I made about your race," Ra whispered almost secretively. "Myth, faith, habit. Control of these gives more power than any weapons." Ra lifted his arms to allow a tunic to be slipped over his head. "Myth, faith, habit," he repeated. "You should remember that.

"Before anyone finds the courage to question my authority, you will grant me a simple request. You will kill your companions for me. You will prove that I am the supreme ruler."

"And if I refuse?" Daniel blurted out.

Calmly, Ra explained the alternative. "Then I shall have to destroy you and all who have seen you. There can only be one Ra," he purred as he tore Catherine's gold medallion from Daniel's neck.

Even though Skaara hadn't told her anything, Sha'uri knew something had happened to Daniel. Otherwise, he would have come back to her. She knew he had been displeased that the elders had wanted him to marry her, but there was still a bond between them. They had found the secret catacomb together, and uncovered the forgotten history of her people. Daniel was her true friend.

When night fell, Sha'uri lit a candle and went down into the underground cell they had explored together. Remembering how Daniel explained the hieroglyphs to her, she read and reread her people's history. Now Sha'uri understood why Ra had forbidden writing in all forms. It was too powerful. Of course, Ra wanted to hide the truth of his beginnings. He had not truly been born in the sun, a child of the gods. He was originally only a mortal man.

18
IN THE BEGINNING

The original species of the stranger now called Ra had had nothing in common with the human species or with this human body he had taken over. They had had nothing in their nature like sympathy, love, or kindness. They focused on survival and possessions. After thousands of years, their arts, sciences, and knowledge seemed unending, yet they lacked wisdom.

As the stranger's race expired, he was millions of light years away from home, searching desperately for a new body. He had mastered the technology to transfer himself into another being but he had to choose carefully. Not only would he inhabit the body, but he would inherit the personality traits of his chosen host.

Ra's childhood proved to be an excellent preparation for the life that was ahead of him. It allowed him to walk toward the blinding light while the rest of his tribe took shelter. For all practical purposes he had been an orphan: his mother a lunatic, his father worse—a violent outcast who wandered the desert by himself. From infancy, the boy had belonged to everyone and to no one.

He was not an especially lovable child, so no one took care to touch or talk to the boy. While families slept together warmly in tents, Ra slept alone. He grew up with something of an animal streak in him. He was slow to trust and quick to attack.

As Ra got older, he was taught by the old one, the leader of the tribe. He hated being kept away from the hunt in order to practise magic in the caves.

He felt alone in every possible way, and resented everyone around him. That night when the brilliant and frightening lights came across the midnight sky, he had no idea what might happen to him, but he was prepared for any fate other than his own.

The boy Ra's hatred for his own people proved useful. When he became the pharaoh, he felt no guilt or remorse as he put his people to hard labor. In fact, he felt a strange new pleasure, which was the most powerful trait the new Ra took from the host body. Ra was now merged with the stranger; together they became the Sun God, to be feared and worshipped.

The pharaoh-god learned quickly how to govern this species. First came the lesson of violence. He must be able to destroy his opponents—not only he, himself, but his soldiers and elite guards. They had to understand that if he ordered them, they would cut their own throats. Ra only rarely tested them.

Ra taught himself to wage war by suppressing the few inevitable, but brief, slave uprisings. He learned to strike back with devastating, merciless strength. He became very good at violence.

The second lesson concerned the psychology of governing. After acquiring an iron fist, he learned how to wrap it in a velvet glove. While violence brought immediate results, myth, faith, and habit were stronger, more durable weapons.

The pharaoh Ra understood the fears and weaknesses of the people and played upon them, ruthlessly. In public he always wore his now-famous mask. Only his private entourage would be privileged to see the human face of Ra.

His guards, too, called upon the fears of the people. The pharaoh's champion defender wore the mask of a jackal, disguised as Anubis, the jackal-headed boatsman who took men's souls to hell. Ra's many Horus guards put on hawklike heads. All played their parts in an intricate web of mythology woven by the master himself, Ra, Sun God.

Now, in Ra's body, the stranger experienced dreams for the first time. Some were disturbing, some pleasant and comforting. It was a strange new sensation, one which he liked very much.

A vision came to him of a vast underground chamber

with magnificently painted walls. In the middle of the room stood an enormous balance scale. Ra himself sat in one of its dishes. Suddenly thousands of people were lining up to test their weight against his. The scales did not measure the physical weight of a body, but the worth of a person's soul, or *Ka*.

One at a time, the people climbed into the dish. But Ra could manipulate the scale at will, tipping it in his favor. When the people became suspicious, they piled onto the scale all together. But, no matter how many people were in the dish on the other side, the scale indicated that the slender boy's *Ka* was worthier.

Ra was beginning to believe his own mythology.

At the same time Ra was learning to govern his slave population, people from far and wide across the desert became subject to powerful, beautiful, and disturbing dreams. In their dreams, the sun itself split open to deliver a living god to them. Night after night, this awesome event took place on a rocky plateau near the banks of a great river.

From the south, the Nubians and the Sudanese followed the banks of the Nile searching for the landscape of the dream. Out of the west from the Sahara, from as far north as Syria and Palestine, they set out. On the backs of camels or behind herds of goats, they came carrying spices, spears, and children. They came speaking no common language, sharing nothing in common except their dream.

Scratching pictures in the dirt and speaking with their hands, they exchanged tales along the way of the lengths they had come and the dangers they had faced. Wave upon wave, they wandered to the base of the plateau, and as each new group arrived and told of their journey, all the desert people took hope that the miraculous dream would be made real.

As powerful as their blazing dream had been, they weren't prepared for the stunning majesty of what actually happened. As they slept along the banks of the river, a shadow blotted out the moon. Soon the winds whipped up and a harsh flood of light poured down on the makeshift camp. They woke and followed the light, running at top speed, fighting for position, yearning to welcome their god to earth.

At the center of the radiance, they found him: the Sun God Ra, his entire body blazing with a feverish golden hue. He was surrounded by a company of kneeling servants. When the servants stood up, the crowds felt spikes of fear pound into their hearts. Each servant had the body of a human but the enormous head of an animal: Khnum, the ram; Sebek, the crocodile; Horus, the hawk; Apis, the bull; Anubis, the jackal; Hathor, the cow; and Ammit, a strange beast known as "the devourer."

Spontaneously, the people laid themselves facedown in the sand and wet grass, weeping, overwhelmed by the miracle.

His worshipers called him Ra-hotep-kan, Sun God, because he had come from the light as bright as the sun. Ra told them that he had conquered Tuat, the land of the dead. He had made servants out of all the animal-gods that lived there. He called upon the people who had answered his call to dedicate their love and their labor to him and his works.

When they died, he told them, they would be escorted to Tuat by his servant Anubis. Each spirit, each *Ka*, would be weighed on a scale. Those who had lived in pious service to Ra would dwell forever in the land of the dead. If not, Ammit the devourer would be waiting nearby.

Construction of Ra's great pyramid began almost at once. The people worked willingly, gratefully, for Ra. They studied, learned, and labored under the supervision of the animal-headed gods. Ra could see that his illiterate, barely civilized subjects were motivated by a mixture of love and fear.

When the structure was nearly complete, Ra transferred a giant ring of quartz, the StarGate, from his spacecraft to a room especially built for it in the pyramid. By that time, however, most of Ra's workers were the sons and daughters of those who had come to the place following the dream. This second generation did not feel the same as their parents about their work on the building. It felt less like sacred labor than like plain old work.

They were less submissive to Ra, and they frequently visited their homelands to speak with those who had not followed the dream. In truth, their nights were spent in hunger and the unsanitary conditions of the sprawling shantytown, while daily they witnessed the outlandish luxury that surrounded their king. They began to want more for themselves.

There was also rumor of a journal that told the truth about Ra's origins. A traitor in Ra's guard leaked its secrets to the young, would-be rebels, who remembered them well as they kept an eye on Ra.

Beginning the night that the pyramid was declared finished, Ra and his bodyguards moved through the crowds selecting hundreds of people to be taken into the pyramid and sent through the StarGate. It was a great honor.

These roundups continued for months. At first, people lined the streets begging to go. Many of the older volunteers were passed over in favor of stronger, younger bodies.

Workers inside the pyramid whispered what they had heard: the chosen people were being forcefully sent through the giant ring to faraway deserts in order to build other pyramids. The slight murmurings of unhappiness made Ra move too quickly, too soon.

Ra's now-frequent trips through the camp soon came to be feared. Children were torn away from their families. Young people slipped out into the desert to escape. Persistent rumors of rebellions on other planets came back through the gate and spread through the city.

Ra began to spend a lot of time away, establishing new settlements on distant planets. He needed more of his quartz mineral, not only to fuel his sarcophagus, which gave him eternal life, but to sustain the technology of his own new civilization. In his absence from earth, he left the discipline to his guards. As people grew more and more unhappy, resistance began to organize.

On his next trip, Ra personally wandered through the mud and stench of the city pointing out those he wanted for the StarGate. Behind the walls of a small mud-brick building, the resistance conspirators were laying their plans. Ra's henchmen, however, paid no attention to their hand-scrawled map of the pyramid's interior. They dragged the men outside and lined them up. But only one of the men was chosen and taken through the gate to the place where Nagada would be founded.

When the signal came that Ra had left, the plotters rushed inside the pyramid, killed the last few of the animal guards, and tore the StarGate down. They could not even scratch it with their hammers and instead dragged it out into the desert and buried it. Months later, when the giant cover stone was carved, they brought it out to bury the gate once and for all. The smashed body of Anubis was already in place.

19
KNOWLEDGE IS POWER

Sha'uri had been down in the catacombs for hours when Skaara, Nabeh, Rabhi, and Aksah came looking for her. She was sitting in the small painted chamber mourning Daniel. When she heard the boys coming, she got up to tell them to leave her alone. But when she saw them in the doorway, she knew what she had to do. She motioned them to sit around her. Then she recited for them the long-hidden history of their people.

As Sha'uri read the words and explained the pictures on the walls, her voice grew more confident. And in that hour, the shepherd boys became men. Knowledge is power and the story of their past made the boys strong.

For Skaara, the story bore out what he had suspected all along. His questions were answered and his doubts erased. He became angry then, angry about all his people killed by Ra's soldiers, angry that they lived their lives not in service to a god but as fools and slaves. He swore that even if it took the rest of his life, he would free his people from Ra.

The preparations for the ceremony had been underway all night. Before dawn a huge caravan set out from Nagada, led by Kasuf. When the three suns rose in the sky, a thousand people were gathered around the entrance of the pyramid.

Huge red silk curtains hung over the pyramid door. As the crowd fell silent, the curtains were pulled back. The surviving American soldiers stumbled out onto the stone ramp, followed by two Horus guards carrying long weapons. Only four members of the team were still alive: O'Neil, Kawalsky, Feretti, and Freeman. One of the Horus guards struck Freeman with his weapon, knocking him to his knees. The other soldiers kneeled, too, before the guard could force them down as well.

Below them Sha'uri pushed her way to the front. Like most of the crowd, she wore a long pale robe with a hood pulled over her face. She made eye contact with both Skaara and Nabeh, who were standing on opposite sides of the ramp. Then she gazed up at the soldiers. Her expression sad and anxious, she wondered where Daniel was, afraid his absence could only mean one thing.

The red curtain opened again. This time a girl of about nine came walking out onto the ramp. She wore a snow-white linen tunic, and a jeweled collar round her neck. It was her job to tell the drummers from Nagada to begin playing.

The girl had lived with Ra in the pyramid palace since she was a tiny baby. It was the first time she had seen the outside. She gazed down at an old man and gasped in horror. In a flash, she realized what it was to grow old. Trembling all over, she ordered the drummers to begin.

As the drumming started, more of Ra's child-servants came out of the doorway. Behind them, the curtain was pulled back to reveal a tall golden throne set on four long poles. Four Horus guards carried the throne out into the sunlight.

Now the fearless jackal-headed warrior, Anubis, stepped through the doorway. He was clutching Daniel by the arm. The soldiers, still on their knees, glanced at one another in shock. O'Neil looked as if he'd seen a ghost.

"You told us he was dead," Kawalsky snarled.

"He was," O'Neil replied. He stared at Daniel. Something was very wrong. He had seen Daniel's chest torn apart before his eyes. No human being could receive a wound like that and live. Perhaps the Daniel Jackson standing next to Anubis was an imposter, O'Neil thought. Some sort of illusion Ra had created. He tried to catch Daniel's eye, but Daniel only looked away.

Sha'uri was also trying to catch Daniel's eye. As soon as she had spotted him, her heart had leaped. She turned first to Skaara and then to Nabeh and gave them each a nod. The two boys squeezed through the crowd, moving into position.

Anubis tapped his staff on the ground. It was time for the ceremony to begin. Kasuf hobbled out. The old man was clearly in pain, but he had dared not stay away for fear of angering Ra. Stretching his arms above his head, Kasuf sang a prayer in honor of the god. *"Ra sa' adam y'emallah, nhet!"* he cried.

"Ra sa' adam," the crowd dutifully repeated.

As if responding to popular demand, a golden figure slowly stepped out from the darkness of the pyramid. It was Ra in his splendid golden disguise. He glided into the light, the sun's rays turning him into a dazzling, floating vision. The crowd gasped as their god sat down on his throne.

Anubis left Daniel's side and approached the throne. Kneeling before Ra, he offered the god-king his weapon. Ra gently refused it, then rising to his feet he dramatically pointed at Daniel. Anubis nodded and walked over to Daniel again.

The crowd knew what would happen next. The travelers were about to be killed. The crowd was not happy, but they dared not show their feelings. "Ra! Ra!" they chanted with one voice.

Meanwhile, Skaara was trying desperately to get Daniel's attention. He coughed, he scratched his head. He even pretended to sneeze. But Daniel didn't look up. Skaara's heart began to beat faster. He had to get Daniel to notice him, and there wasn't much time.

Anubis thrust the long weapon into Daniel's hands. Daniel took it. His face was expressionless. But his mind was churning. What should he do? He might not be best friends with the other team members, but he couldn't kill them. Yet even if he refused to pull the trigger, the soldiers were as good as dead. So was he. Then Ra would surely keep his promise and kill everyone who had seen the visitors. That meant Kasuf, Skaara, Nabeh, Sha'uri, and the others would all die.

The worst part was he had no one but himself to blame. When General West showed Daniel the second StarGate, he knew getting the team back home wasn't a sure thing. But he had gambled because he wanted to make the journey so badly. Now all these people would have to pay for his selfishness. Daniel's hands tightened around the weapon in his hands. What should he do? He had to make a decision.

Daniel blinked. Something was reflecting the sunlight into his eyes. Someone's jewelry perhaps or a shiny button. He blinked again. How ridiculous that something so small should bother him when so many lives were in danger. He glanced down into the crowd and spotted Skaara. The boy was using O'Neil's lighter to reflect the sun up at him. Daniel's eyes widened.

Skaara, seeing he had Daniel's attention, opened his coat. Under it was hidden one of the rifles from the base camp.

Daniel nodded to show he understood. Raising his weapon, he shouted to the crowd in their language:

"There is only one Ra! Ra orders me to kill these men, my brothers. Ra is always right! I will obey him unto death." Getting into the act, Daniel pointed his finger at the soldiers, thundering how evil they had been to challenge the divine Ra. Then he aimed his weapon at O'Neil.

As he was about to fire, Daniel whipped around to face the pyramid entrance. Closing his eyes, he squeezed the trigger. The laser beam tore through the air with a terrifying whine. Before it even hit, O'Neil was on his feet. With a few quick blows, the colonel disarmed the nearest Horus guard.

Skaara and the other shepherd boys pulled out their weapons, too, and fired at Ra and his soldiers. Surrounded by his children, Ra retreated at once to the safety of the pyramid.

O'Neil had already killed one Horus, and disarmed another, but more were coming. Freeman heaved the wounded Feretti onto his shoulders, and hauled him to the edge of the stone ramp. Anubis fired on them from behind. Freeman was struck in the head, and died instantly. Kawalsky managed to scoop up Feretti and race off into the crowd.

People were milling around in all directions. Anubis looked everywhere, but he could see no trace of Daniel or the soldiers. He soon guessed correctly what had happened. They had been disguised in long hooded robes, so that they looked just like the rest of the crowd. Anubis called for the glider pilots. He told them to go out at once and search for the soldiers. Soon two uda-jeets were gliding low over the crowd, staring into each and every face, and killing anyone who looked the least bit suspicious.

Even in disguise Kawalsky should have been an easy target. Not only was he taller than anyone else in Nagada, but he was carrying the wounded Feretti on his back. But the shepherd boys hustled him and Feretti across the sand, hiding them in a herd of mastadges, along with Daniel and O'Neil.

Skaara helped O'Neil and Daniel mount Little Bit. Nabeh hoisted Kawalsky and Feretti onto another mas-tadge. Next Skaara sent the herd racing out across the dunes. There were twelve mastadges in all, two to carry the soldiers to safety and ten to act as decoys for the udajeets.

At first, it looked as if the shepherd boy's escape plan would work. Followed by the herd, Little Bit and the other mastadge went galloping toward the safety of Nagada. But then the udajeets spotted the animals. Peering down at them for a moment, the pilots chose two to chase.

20
NOWHERE TO RUN

Ra sat on his throne, seething like a basket of vipers. The udajeet pilots, a pair of Horus guards, marched in. They kneeled before their master. "Where are they?" Ra hissed, his amber eyes alight.

"They vanished."

"What do you mean, vanished?"

"A sandstorm came and we lost them." The pilot couldn't keep the fear out of his voice. "But surely the storm will kill them."

Ra was beyond furious. But no trace of his rage showed on the surface. He merely strolled over to a jeweled box sitting on a table. Out of the box, he took a coin-sized quartz jewel with gold wires coming from it. The wires fitted Ra's hand like an elegant glove. Ra turned back to the pilots.

"Do not be afraid." He walked toward the pilot who had spoken. "I know you tried." But as the pilot relaxed, Ra's gloved hand flew out at the man's face. When the pilot saw the gleaming quartz he knew his life was over. Ra touched the pilot's cheek.

The dark jewel came to life. The pilot's head began to shake violently, then his features themselves seemed to turn liquid. The glove's jewel worked in the same way as the StarGate. But here the quartz was put to a much more evil use. As Ra held the jewel to the man's head, he was actually rearranging his molecules, melting him down from the inside. A moment later it was over. Ra calmly stood up and turned toward the other pilot.

Hurricane force winds blasted across the desert. Fighting through the whirling sand, O'Neil and Daniel clung to Little Bit. Daniel stumbled and fell. The mastadge turned around and howled even louder than the wind. Pulling back his hood, O'Neil fumbled around until he found Daniel, already half-buried in the sand.

O'Neil was starting to dig Daniel out, when he saw that Little Bit was taking off. "Hey, wait!" O'Neil shrieked. But Little Bit was gone. O'Neil knew it would not be long before he and Daniel were completely buried alive in the sand.

Half an hour later, Little Bit came trundling back. Up to their noses in sand, Daniel and O'Neil stared at her, amazed. Then they saw the group of helmeted figures around her. One came scrambling up to them, pulling off his helmet and protective mask. It was Nabeh, the bucktoothed shepherd boy. Next to him was Skaara, decked out in the uniform of a United States Marine. He squinted at O'Neil and gestured—thumbs up.

His eyes swollen shut, Daniel was helped by the shepherd boys up the rocky hillside to the cave entrance. O'Neil walked behind them. When Kawalsky saw who it was, he lowered his rifle and helped them inside.

A dozen or so boys were in the cave, buttoned into the oversized camouflage uniforms they'd rescued from the base camps. Stacked against the walls were two dozen rifles and several crates of ammunition. Halfway back, a makeshift hospital had been set up. Sha'uri, her face bandaged, was doctoring Feretti.

"You made it!" Kawalsky greeted O'Neil with a roar. "With some help," O'Neil replied, continuing into the cave. He noticed that Skaara and Nabeh were following him, as if they were his personal bodyguards. O'Neil eyed them doubtfully. In his view, they were way too young be wearing U.S. Marine uniforms.

"What do you think, Colonel?" Kawalsky asked. "They're not exactly special forces, but they're real eager to enlist."

"Take the guns away from them before they hurt themselves."

"Come again, sir?"

"You heard me, Kawalsky. Take the guns and send them home."

Kawalsky felt like exploding. He was fed up with O'Neil coming into situations he didn't understand, situations Kawalsky had completely under control, and messing everything up.

"There's nowhere for them to go." He forced himself to stay cool. "If they go back to the city, they'll be killed for helping us. Besides, we could sure use the help, sir."

"For *what*?" O'Neil got in his face, suddenly furious. "To do *what*, Lieutenant?"

O'Neil's outburst caught everyone by surprise. "To get back through the StarGate and safely home," said Kawalsky, dazed. He was bewildered that his superior officer had forgotten the goal of their mission.

Daniel, who understood the source of the confusion, called out to O'Neil, "Why don't you just tell them the truth? Tell them about the bomb."

"What's he talking about, Colonel?"

"My orders were simple. I was to send you home, then search for any signs of possible danger to earth. If I found any, I was supposed to blow up the StarGate. Well, guess what. I found some."

"Why wasn't I told!" Now Kawalsky was furious.

"It was strictly need-to-know," O'Neil replied using the Marine slang for classified information.

"Need-to-know? Don't you think this is something I would need to know!?"

Frustrated, Daniel interjected, "And this *great* plan of

yours was for us to leave you here with a nuclear weapon. Well, it's *his* now and tomorrow he's going to send it back through the gate along with a shipment of the quartz mineral they mine here. Apparently, when the bomb goes off, this shipment will detonate and cause an explosion a hundred times more powerful than that bomb alone is capable of."

"He told you all this?" O'Neil asked skeptically.

"Yes."

"All right then," O'Neil stepped forward, in command. "I'll intercept the bomb before he can send it through."

"Colonel, listen to me," Daniel pressed. "It's not the bomb, it's the StarGate on earth that poses the threat. Think about it. As long as it is up and functional, he'll always have access. The StarGate on earth is what we have to shut down!"

O'Neil hissed back, "You're absolutely right, but thanks to you, we don't have that option, do we?" He stood up and walked as far toward the mouth of the cave as the sandstorm would allow, and sat down.

"I *knew* it all along," Feretti broke the silence, "this was a suicide mission."

Daniel stared at O'Neil, sitting at the mouth of the cave. The colonel hadn't moved for a half an hour. Daniel frowned and went over to him. "Sir?"

"What do you want, Jackson?"

"So, you've accepted the fact you'll never go home?"

Daniel asked. O'Neil just shrugged. Daniel tried again. "Don't you have people you care about? Don't you have a family?"

"I had a family." O'Neil's voice was hollow. "No one should ever have to outlive their own child."

Daniel knew better than to try to talk O'Neil out of his pain. When his parents had died, there was nothing anyone could say. Still, he had to do something. If the colonel didn't care whether he survived the mission or not, they were all doomed.

Daniel tried one more time. "Colonel, listen. I don't want to die. Your men don't want to die. These kids helping us don't want to die either. It's a shame you're in such a hurry to."

The words hit O'Neil like a punch to the stomach. He looked up. But Daniel was already walking away. Skaara tiptoed up to him, carrying a bowl of stew. The boy offered it to O'Neil with a smile. The colonel waved him away. Skaara was puzzled. He sniffed the stew. It smelled pretty good for cave cooking.

The boy slid the bowl closer and pantomimed eating. O'Neil shook his head. "I don't *want* it!"

Skaara clucked like a chicken and flapped his wings, as he'd seen Daniel do. "Bock, bock, bock?" he said encouragingly.

O'Neil couldn't help cracking a smile. "Chicken, right!"

"Shicken!" The boy looked so pleased with himself, O'Neil caved in.

"Okay." He took the bowl.

As O'Neil ate, his mind went back again to the day J.J. had died. He seemed to see himself walking into his son's room. "J.J.? J.J.? Where are you?" Then he heard the siren. He hoped it was going somewhere else, but it drew ever closer. He went down the hall past his bedroom, and saw that the drawer of the nightstand—the drawer that was always supposed to be locked—was wide open. His gun! He raced out into the backyard, and saw Sarah, with J.J. lying on the ground in front of her. There was blood all over him. O'Neil remembered what the ambulance man had said: "It's a damn shame, kids playing with guns." O'Neil cradled his son in his arms, rocking him back and forth. After that, he didn't want to move anymore, speak anymore, live anymore. He was glad when General West's officers showed up with this mission. It meant he didn't have to go on.

O'Neil shook his head and returned to the present. Skaara was beside him, staring up at him with a look of admiration.

Daniel walked up to Sha'uri, who was stirring the stew. "Need any help?" he asked her. At his words, Nabeh clutched his stomach and fell backward laughing. *"Bani ne-ateru ani, hee na'a ani-ben!"* the boy sputtered.

It took Daniel a moment to understand his meaning. *A husband doing this kind of work! Ridiculous!* Daniel turned red. "A husband!" He looked at Sha'uri. "This crazy boy here just called me your husband!"

153

Daniel meant it as a joke, but Sha'uri turned and fled to the back of the cave. Daniel followed her. "Hey, wait!"

Sha'uri turned on him, her eyes huge. "I'm sorry," she said. "Don't be angry. I didn't tell them."

"Tell them what?"

"That you did not want me for a wife."

In the flickering light, Sha'uri looked more than ever like Daniel's beautiful Egyptian statue. He leaned toward her. The next thing he knew, Daniel Jackson, the biggest romantic failure of all time, was kissing her as hard as he could.

When Daniel woke up the next morning, he could see Sha'uri and the shepherd boys still sleeping in army sleeping bags all around him. A grin spread over his face. He stood up, stretching his legs. Skaara was already awake, and was busy doing something at the mouth of the cave. Daniel lifted his head to look. Inspired by the pictures in the catacomb, Skaara was using a piece of soft red stone to draw a story of his own. Daniel's grin widened. The kid was no Rembrandt, but he was trying. He had drawn a wobbly pyramid, with three suns above it. Around it were stick figures firing guns at the animal-headed soldiers standing in the pyramid doorway.

Daniel looked at Skaara's drawing in amusement. Suddenly, his chest felt tight. He realized the importance of what he was watching. Skaara was writing. He was recording the history of his people for the first time in centuries. Daniel was watching the dawn of a new ancient Egyptian culture.

It was a perfect moment. And it gave Daniel a new-found sense of responsibility. Skaara's talents as a historian must be allowed to live and grow. But for that to happen, Daniel and the soldiers must first face Ra.

Daniel stared at Skaara's drawing, watching as the sun lit up the rough red lines on the cave wall. Suddenly, he leaped toward the drawing. "That's it! The point of origin!"

"Jackson, what're you doing?" Kawalsky opened his eyes.

Daniel was madly digging through the fire for a half-burnt stick. "The point of origin!" Stick in hand, Daniel traced a line over the top of the Skaara's drawing, connecting the three suns over the pyramid. "That's it! I saw that symbol on the StarGate here. Three suns above the pyramid."

Everyone was awake now, staring at Daniel.

"I found it! The seventh symbol! We're going home!"

21
THE TROJAN HORSE

On days when the quartz was to be shipped, every working person in Nagada was expected to go to the mining pit. They labored for two or three easy hours, loading up the carts with the precious ore. Then the quartz was carried to the pyramid and sent through the StarGate. When this was done, the city celebrated the feast of Tekfallit. Prayers and songs thanking Ra for all he provided were followed by a citywide feast. The celebrations usually lasted late into the night.

But today was no ordinary Tekfallit. Ra had not ruled for so long without learning when to be cautious. On this Tekfallit, only a thousand workers were allowed into the mine. Watched over by Ra's cruellest Horus guard, they were driven without mercy. Ra needed only one guard to control so many, because the workers believed the myths they'd been taught since birth. To them the Horus guard was not a mortal but a god.

Finally, all but the last cart were loaded and ready to go. However, the loading of this cart was taking longer than the Horus guard thought it should. Cracking his long whip, Ra's hawk-headed henchman made it clear to the exhausted workers that they'd better hurry or else.

At last, one of workers collapsed at the base of the ladder leading up to the carts. Raising his whip high, the Horus struck the man full force. The man tried to stand, but stumbled back down into the sand again. Furious, the Horus guard unsheathed his dagger and advanced on the worker. He planned to teach the others a gruesome lesson, demonstrating what would happen to those who shirked their duties.

Suddenly, the man rolled onto his back, showing the Horus the business end of a U.S. Marine rifle. The exhausted worker was none other than Colonel Jack O'Neil. O'Neil stared up at the Horus and cocked his rifle. Several other miners, also pulled rifles from beneath their robes. The Horus dropped his whip.

Kasuf, drawn by the noise, dashed down the cliff's side. When he saw what was happening, he flew into a panic. Shouting and pointing, Kasuf got the attention of all the miners in the pit.

"Hey, Jackson," O'Neil yelled. "What's he saying?"

"He's telling them that they have to stop us," Daniel replied. "That Ra will kill everyone who disobeys. If they help us, they will anger the gods."

"Anger the gods, huh?" O'Neil eyed the Horus guard with scorn, making it clear he wasn't impressed. Almost casually, he turned his back on the hawk-headed warrior, giving the god a chance to pull his weapon. The Horus took it, raising his dagger high. It was a big mistake. O'Neil wheeled around and fired. The blast hit the warrior's armored chestplate, knocking him six feet backward. He fell in a heap in the sand.

"*Naaah!*" Kasuf screamed as if he were the one who'd been shot. O'Neil turned to his troops. "Okay, let's get to the carts," he boomed, leading the way toward the base of the cliff.

Daniel hesitated. He could see by the miners shocked expressions that they didn't understand what had happened. As far as they were concerned, O'Neil had killed one of their gods. They were terrified of what Ra would do to them now. Daniel knew that to win the people's support, the team had to make them understand that Ra and his soldiers were not gods but tyrants.

"Wait!" Daniel ran over to the Horus's limp body and pressed the button at the base of his helmet. The chilling helmet slowly slid back, folding itself into the golden collar around the man's neck. Beneath the mask was the unremarkable face of Ra's cruellest warrior. Except for his armor, he could have belonged to any family in the city.

"Take a look at your god!" Daniel shouted in ancient Egyptian. "He is a man like any other!"

An excited murmur spread like a brush fire through

the crowd, as they took in Daniel's words. In that moment, the people saw clearly. They understood now that Ra was not a god, but merely a cruel leader, someone they could fight.

Daniel marched back to O'Neil and the others. Now, most of the Nagadans were on his side. As he passed, they called out words of congratulation and encouragement. Sha'uri beamed at him. Then her expression changed to one of horror. The Horus was on his feet! O'Neil's bullet had only hit the guard's armor, knocking him unconscious. He charged toward Daniel, swinging a pickax.

Daniel pointed his rifle and fired. The shot landed under the man's armored breastplate. He fell down dead. Daniel felt sick. He had never killed anyone before.

"Not so easy is it?" O'Neil took the gun out of Daniel's trembling hands.

The caravan was heading out, but Sha'uri was nowhere to be seen. From his perch on the first cart, which was being pulled by Little Bit, Daniel looked around for her. At last he spotted her. She was arguing with Kasuf. The old man was obviously pleading with her not to go with the rebels. Daniel watched with mixed feelings. On the one hand, he wanted Sha'uri with them. She had helped plan the attack and deserved to be there. On the other, he wanted her to stay behind and be safe.

Sha'uri herself was also torn over what to do. She

loved Kasuf, her father, and had always obeyed him. But now he was telling her that she must continue to serve Ra. In her heart, she knew that was impossible. She looked up and saw Daniel turning his head to stare back at her. "Sha'uri!" he called.

In that moment her decision was made. Almost sadly, she twisted free of Kasuf. "It is better to die on your feet than live on your knees," she told him. Then she turned and ran to join Daniel and the others.

Ra stared out the great window of his pyramid craft, watching the caravan of quartz crawl across the sea of sand. This caravan looked exactly the same as countless others he'd watched. But was it? A smile flickered across Ra's face. He realized he was glad the earthling with the glasses had escaped. It made everything more interesting. There was even a chance he was part of this caravan, disguised no doubt as one of the miners.

Ra turned away from the window and called for his guards. Seconds later, two Horuses knelt before him, awaiting his orders.

"Take the tray with the captured earthling supplies to the StarGate room," Ra commanded. "Then go meet the shipment."

The bomb would be sent to earth with the shipment, Ra thought with satisfaction. After taking his revenge on all of earth, he would exact it from the escaped soldiers.

The same ceremony was always observed before the quartz shipment was taken into the pyramid. Skaara knew that if the team strayed from custom in any way, Ra's guards would notice. What was more, O'Neil had put him in charge of getting the team inside. Skaara ordered the team of caravans to stop at the base of the stone ramp. Then he kneeled and sang in a strong clear voice: *"Atema en-Ra Hallam a'ana t'yon shaknowm assar Atem Re."* Ra, who comes from the sun, we now gratefully give you the results of our work. Holy sun god Ra!

When the song was finished, Skaara turned to Nabeh and noticed something under his friend's hood.

"What is that?"

"What is what?" Nabeh acted innocent.

"Under your hood. It's the green hat, isn't it?"

Nabeh grinned. Everyone had told him he couldn't bring the helmet. But he couldn't bear to leave his treasure behind.

"It isn't funny," Skarra told him. "If they find the green hat, they will kill us."

Nabeh's eyes filled with dread as he gazed toward the pyramid entrance. Three armed Horus guards had stepped out onto the ramp. Not knowing what else to do, Skaara ordered the delivery crew to kneel at once in respect to the gods. At last, he rose and unharnessed Little Bit, handing the reins to Nabeh. "Keep the hat covered or we will all die!" Skaara whispered, motioning to the others to wheel this first cart up the ramp.

Now, a new problem lifted its huge, ugly head. It was Little Bit. Nabeh had insisted on putting the clumsy mastadge at the head of the caravan. The others hadn't been sure it was a good idea, but now they saw it was an even worse one than they had thought. As the cart was pulled away, Little Bit began to bellow loudly, wanting to follow Daniel, who was hidden inside it. Nabeh tried desperately to quiet the beast, but the stubborn animal kept blubbering.

The commotion made the lead Horus suspicious. "Stop, where you are," he shouted at the workers. "Put out your hands!"

The hooded workers all held their hands straight out in front of them. The Horus marched up and down, looking them over suspiciously. He stopped at Nabeh, who was still pleading with Little Bit to shut up. For one horrible moment, Skaara was sure the Horus was going to ask his dim-witted friend to uncover his head. But at last the Horus moved on and motioned for the workers to go on into the pyramid.

The first cart and workers vanished inside. But as the second cart was starting up the ramp, Little Bit, still longing for Daniel, let out an earsplitting howl.

The lead Horus signaled the second cart to stop, then he and his two henchmen went inside after the first one. Everyone watching knew this meant trouble.

"I knew this Trojan Horse plan was no good," Feretti muttered. "Should we go after them?"

"Just wait," Kawalsky replied. "It still might work."

Inside the pyramid, the three Horuses surrounded the cart. The lead Horus pulled back the first worker's hood, revealing the face of a frightened shepherd boy. He slammed the boy to the floor, then moved on to the next worker. It was Sha'uri. She shrieked as the Horus tore out a handful of her hair. Ra's henchmen stopped and stared, shocked to see a woman.

But that shock was nothing compared to the one the Horuses got a second later, as Daniel and O'Neil rose out of the pile of quartz. Lifting their weapons, the two men aimed and started firing. The shepherd boys joined in, pulling rifles from beneath their robes. Shots ricochetted through the hall. Unfortunately, both Daniel and O'Neil chose the lead Horus as their target. He was stopped permanently by their bullets, but that gave the other two time to slip away into the shadows.

"Get inside, everybody!" Kawalsky howled. The door to the pyramid, a giant stone slab, was closing from above! Following Kawalsky's lead, the workers sprinted frantically up the ramp. Fast, but not fast enough. Kawalsky turned to see Nabeh racing up beside him. He spotted the boy's helmet. Grabbing it off Nabeh's head, Kawalsky flung it at the door like a Frisbee. Strike! The helmet lodged in place, holding the door open a few inches. "Fetch some wood from the carts. We'll try to lever it back up," Kawalsky shouted.

Daniel blinked. O'Neil was gone. He had been there a second before, firing at the Horus guards, but now he had vanished. The entrance hall felt eerily silent. Daniel, unused to warfare, breathed a sigh of relief. Maybe Ra's henchman had given up. He took Sha'uri's arm, and signaled to the shepherd boys to retreat behind the pillars.

This was exactly the mistake Ra's guards wanted them to make. While the space behind the pillars was dark, the light from the windows silhouetted them there. As Daniel and Sha'uri crouched down, a Horus guard crept toward them from behind. The guard slowly raised his weapon, preparing to fire. Just then the silence was shattered by a scream.

It was Sha'uri. She had spotted the glint of the Horus's quartz-powered weapon. The shot went wild, streaking the air six inches above Daniel's head. Daniel hit the floor. He realized that there must be Horus guards lurking everywhere in the shadows, with more riding the medallion down from the spaceship above.

"One, two, three, lift!" Kawalsky grunted. The two soldiers and six shepherd boys jammed their shoulders against the planks of wood, trying to jimmy up the huge stone slab. They had now raised the door six inches above the helmet.

"No, not yet!" Kawalsky shouted, as Skaara shimmied under it. But the boy was gone. Nabeh leaned down and scooped up his precious helmet, grinning as he showed Kawalsky his prize.

"Put it back. We need that there!" Kawalsky roared. Either Nabeh didn't understand or he pretended not to.

Sticking the helmet on his head, he went back to trying to lift the door.

Squinting in the darkness, Skaara let out a sharp, short whistle. Sha'uri lifted her head and spotted her half brother under the door. The whistle was a signal they had used since childhood. Sha'uri realized the door was open. They must seize their chance to make their escape. She gathered the shepherd boys around her, and whispered to them what they must do. The boys swallowed and started running toward the door like scared jackrabbits. One after another, they shimmied out through the opening. Sha'uri was about to join them, when Daniel pulled her back. A Horus guard had his weapon trained on the door. The children were safe, but Daniel and Sha'uri were stuck where they were.

The huge stone door seemed to be getting heavier. Using the last of their strength, Kawalsky and Feretti held it up as the last shepherd boy came wriggling out under it. Kawalsky was about to let the door drop, when he saw that Skaara had gone back into the pyramid. "Get back here!" he howled.

"Lieutenant, I can't hold it up any more," Feretti grunted pitifully.

"Just keep holding." Kawalsky ordered him.

Daniel and Sha'uri held their breath as a Horus guard strode past them. They didn't know it, but a second Horus was moving in on them from the other side. He was already close enough to get a good shot at them, but he wanted to be sure of killing them both.

He aimed his weapon at Daniel's blond head. But the shot that rang out was not his. The laser exploded through his helmet, sending him spinning into the shadows. When the smoke cleared, Daniel and Sha'uri saw that it was O'Neil who had fired.

It was the first time Daniel had ever been happy to see the colonel. He started to say so, but O'Neil put his finger up to his lips. Just then Skaara screamed.

O'Neil hit the ground, just missing getting hit in the head. Another Horus guard was hiding behind the cart of quartz. Skaara had spotted him just in time. Daniel and Sha'uri rolled to one side, O'Neil to the other. The Horus fired again. The shot sailed over them, hitting the stone door above Skaara. The door slammed down like a thunderclap.

Thinking Skaara had been killed, a white-hot rage flooded O'Neil—all the anger he had never been able to express when his own son died. Now he would make the Horus pay for both deaths. Firing madly, he advanced on the cart that hid the hawk-headed warrior.

The Horus calmly waited until O'Neil was almost on him to take his shot. He aimed for the colonel's head. But by luck or instinct, O'Neil ducked just as the shot was about to strike. Now he knew exactly where the Horus was. Raising his weapon, he blasted the hawk between the eyes.

Outside Kawalsky held Skaara up by one ankle. *"Don't ever do that again!"* he thundered. The laser blast had shattered the wooden plank Kawalsky was using as a lever. Without Kawalsky's strength to hold it up, the door had come down in a hurry. But not before he managed to yank Skaara to safety.

Skaara, hanging upside down, opened his mouth and shouted a single word. "Udajeet!" Ra's gliders were flying overhead.

Kawalsky dropped the boy. "Scatter!" he shouted. As the shepherd boys scrambled for cover, Kawalsky made a dash for the obelisks. He was hoping to make himself a target, giving the others a chance to get away. The big man looked over his shoulder. Two gliders were bearing down on him. Both pilots fired. At the hiss of their lasers, Kawalsky veered off the ramp and swan dived into the dunes, just before the huge ramp was blown to smithereens.

22
CHANGE OF PLANS

Ra was an expert game-player. He had taught himself to play every kind of game well. And he was a very bad loser. At this moment, Ra was amusing himself by playing two games at once. First, he was playing an ancient Egyptian board game called Senet. Second, he was plotting how to crush the annoying earthlings.

He was playing Senet, known as the chess of the pharaohs, against a thirteen-year-old boy, his favorite among his child slaves. The boy was an intelligent player, but Ra knew he could easily defeat him. So he gave himself a handicap: he only gazed at the game pieces—pyramids and obelisks—every other move.

Ra had also given himself a handicap in his contest against the earthlings and the rebels. He had chosen his shyest slave, a girl of nine, to sit at the pyramid window and tell him what was happening below. The girl had a bad stutter, and now her fear and excitement made her almost impossible to understand.

As far as Ra was concerned, the handicaps made the games more of a challenge. Not only was he going to win both contests, he was going to do it with one arm tied behind his back.

Ra took the boy's pyramid with his obelisk, a move that put the game squarely in his control. He had just ordered the udajeet to go shoot down the rebels. Soon victory would be his in both contests. Ra glanced at the boy. But to his great annoyance, the child was not there. He had gone to the window to watch the fighting below. "Is this how you serve me?" Ra shrieked. He reached forward as if to slap the boy, then turned to Anubis instead. "Go, kill them," he hissed. "Kill them all."

Carrying his last flare, O'Neil tiptoed toward the StarGate room. He stopped, alarmed. Torches had been lit on either side of the gate, and beside it was a table that hadn't been there before. On the table was a silver tray with captured radios, helmets, guns, books, and the pieces of the bomb on it. O'Neil peered into the room. It was empty! O'Neil could hardly believe their luck. He motioned the others forward.

"Okay, Jackson, fire it up!"

Daniel let go of Sha'uri's hand. Laying down his rifle he took out the notebook with the six symbols he'd copied from the catacomb. Putting his hand on the sliding inner ring of the StarGate, he spun the first symbol into place. He was starting on the second symbol when he felt Sha'uri tug on his arm.

"Kiner onio," she said. When Daniel didn't understand, she pointed at O'Neil. The colonel was putting the bomb back together. Daniel couldn't believe it. They were about to get away, and O'Neil was going to blow them up!

"What are you doing?" Daniel demanded. "I thought we agreed it's the StarGate on earth we have to destroy."

O'Neil kept working. "That's what I'm counting on *you* to do, Jackson," he said. "Get back to the silo and destroy the gate."

"But I thought we agreed to go together—"

"Change of plans, Jackson. I'm staying here."

"You're what? Why?"

"I have to make sure this thing goes off. I'm just completing my mission." O'Neil plunged the orange key into the slot between the bomb's two canisters. He then typed something into the device's keypad and pressed the Enter key. Now the timer was set. 12:00, 12:00, 12:00. The blinking red numbers filled the display panel.

"What about Kawalsky and Feretti? What about her?" Daniel demanded, pointing at Sha'uri.

"Take her with you if you want, but get moving." O'Neil pressed Enter again and the countdown began. 11:59, 11:58, 11:57. Daniel stared at him, flabbergasted. "You're running out of time, Jackson."

The room abruptly exploded with sizzling white light. Someone was firing one of Ra's quartz-powered weapons at them from the doorway. Sha'uri fell down, hit in the chest. Daniel picked up his rifle, firing like a madman. The Horus at the door tumbled down dead. Daniel raced over to Sha'uri. "Please, please let her live long enough so that I can get her through the StarGate to medical help!" he was pleading.

O'Neil was already bent over her. "It's no good, Jackson. She's dead." 11:45, 11:44, 11:43.

"We haven't got a prayer," Feretti said. "They've caught us out here with nowhere to go."

They were crouched in the space between the sand and the side of the ramp, Ra's udajeets still gliding over them, bombarding the area with firepower.

"We're sitting ducks out here. And these guys know it."

"Don't worry," Kawalsky murmurred. "I've got a plan."

"A plan!" Feretti thought this was hilarious. "We're stuck out in the open, under heavy fire, we're totally outgunned, and most of us don't even speak the same language. Whatever you've got I don't think you better call it a plan."

"Okay, you want to see a plan. Watch this!" Kawalsky leaped out of the ditch and tore across the sand, dodging fire bursts as he went.

"Jackson, the gate. There's no time. We've got to get you back to the silo. Jackson?" Daniel hadn't moved. He was still sitting with his arms around Sha'uri. O'Neil knew how he felt, but he had to get Daniel on his feet. "It's over. She's gone. Now get up. We need you to go through that gate."

Outside in the passageway, a stream of blue light shot from the floor of the medallion room up to the ceiling. "Uh-oh," O'Neil said. "Looks like we got company." Daniel stared at the spreading circle of light. Then he thought of something—the sarcophagus. It had brought him back to life. It could do the same for Sha'uri! Lifting her into his arms, he leaped toward the blue light.

"Wait!" O'Neil lunged after them. Yet by the time he made it to the medallion, Daniel and Sha'uri were already vanishing in the blue haze. O'Neil noticed that the blue laser light had cut off the part of Sha'uri's robe not in the circle as neatly as a pair of scissors. "Jackson, what the hell are you doing? The bomb!"

O'Neil thought he saw Daniel's mouth move in reply. "Wait for me!" Then he and Sha'uri were gone. O'Neil turned to check the timer. 11:08.

Thwack! Something smashed into the colonel's jaw, sending him spinning across the floor. When O'Neil looked up, the hair rose on his arms. This was the moment he had known all along would come. Standing over O'Neil was a live version of the twisted fossil he'd seen in the silo: the huge armored creature with the head of a jackal, Ra's champion warrior, Anubis.

Kawalsky strained against the weight of the cart, but couldn't tip it over. When the first two shepherd boys came running out of the dunes to help, he tried to explain his plan to them as quickly as he could. "We're going to turn this cart over, see? Then we're going to go turn that cart over, and build ourselves a fort, okay?"

"Oh-khay!" the boys agreed.

"You didn't understand a word I said, did you?" Maybe the boys didn't, but they knew he needed help. When the coast was clear, Kawalsky and the boys turned the cart belly up, spilling the quartz out into the sand. They dashed over to the second cart. Skaara and Feretti came over to help. When the second cart was upside down, too, everyone ducked underneath it to escape the glider's next attack.

On his hands and knees, Kawalsky tested the weight of the cart. Then, like the great Greek hero Atlas holding up the heavens, he slowly stood up. The others did, too. Carrying the cart over their heads, like a giant turtle shell, they marched between the obelisks. Now they had a new command post.

The other shepherd boys dashed over to join them. But Nabeh was still on top of the crushed ramp, a hundred yards away. The dim-witted boy thought he was safe. He jogged along the ramp toward them. Skaara tried to warn him, but Nabeh didn't seem to hear. A glider came swooping down on him from behind.

"Nabeh! Anda ni. Khem eem!" Jump off! Skaara shouted, then rushed out to his friend's rescue. Before

he could reach him, the glider fired. The ground in front of Nabeh exploded into dust and rocks. Skaara felt a wave of heat pass over him, and when he looked again Nabeh had disappeared.

Skaara took a step forward, then was hauled backward by Kawalsky. Skaara fought to free himself, but the soldier held him tight until the boy stopped struggling.

"We don't have many options," Kawalsky said grimly, "but at least we can concentrate all our firepower at the same target." He pointed to the grenade launcher the boys had rescued from the equipment camp. "If we're lucky, this baby will bring down those toy jets for us!"

Feretti pulled out three grenades. "Not exactly a plan, but close enough." he said. One of the gliders was swooping towards them. "Now!" Kawalsky shouted. Ten rifles plus Feretti at the grenade launcher blasted out from under the overturned cart.

The seemingly minnow-sized jet took a grenade in the tail. It was enough to throw the pilot off course. His wing clipped one of the obelisks, and the craft crashed into the dunes like an out-of-control boomerang, and was devoured in a ball of flame.

The sarcophagus room was empty. Daniel lifted Sha'uri onto the hard bed at the center of the device, then stepped back as the machine whirred to life. He watched as the stone lid softly closed. He had no idea how long the machine would take to bring her back, or even if it needed to be turned on. But he had to try.

Daniel stared at the sarcophagus. On its side, inlaid in gold and jewels was the ancient Egyptian story of Osiris. Hacked to pieces by his enemies, his body was spread over the banks of the Nile. His wife Isis wandered the land, gathering the pieces of Osiris. She put his body together and wrapped it in cloth. And he was reborn. Daniel only hoped it would work for Sha'uri.

He looked up and saw that Ra had come in the room. Ra was wearing his golden disguise, and he shimmered all over. Daniel stared at him, paralyzed.

Ra looked at Daniel, and at the sarcophagus. "Why?" he rasped. "Why come here now? For this?" Ra touched the golden coffin with one golden finger. "Have you put something inside?"

Daniel didn't answer.

Ra smiled and ran his hand slowly over the lid of the machine. His smile widened when he saw how anxious this made Daniel. The coffin lid slid back to show Sha'uri's sleeping face. The scab over her eyebrow, from when Ra's soldiers had burned Nagada, was almost completely healed.

"*Hana'i Hana'e,*" Ra whispered, still smiling. The phrase which Daniel didn't know, meant *How romantic*. Ra's amber eyes met Daniel's "Now you can die together."

O'Neil's instincts took over. Before Anubis could react, the colonel wedged the jackal's staff under his throat, forcing the warrior backward. Slamming him into the wall, he tried to take away his weapon. But Anubis was too strong for him. He shoved O'Neil to the ground, and raised the weapon. O'Neil rolled out of the way—fast. The laser blast landed inches from his head. On his feet again, he dove around the corner into the great hall. Somehow he had to get to the bomb and stop the countdown to give Jackson enough time.

O'Neil crouched in the inky darkness of the great hall, watching the door. He saw Anubis come in, hunting for him. He heard Anubis's footsteps coming closer, and then another strange scraping sound. By the time he figured out what it was, it was too late. The staff which the jackal had been dragging along the floor had caught him in the legs. O'Neil clattered over the staff, but managed to get to his feet again. Guessing in the darkness, he brought down his fist with all his force. It landed with a crack on Anubis's nose. The jackal cried out, letting go of his weapon.

Both warriors dived for it. Back and forth they fought, kicking, punching, and butting heads. O'Neil was using every trick in his book and was barely breaking even. Then he remembered the bomb. Knocking Anubis away, he sprinted back toward the StarGate room. 5:20, 5:19, 5:18.

Kawalsky and his troops were having a rough time. The two remaining gliders had attacked together. The boys, aiming at the first, hadn't seen the second coming up behind them. Five of them had been killed. Now, the survivors had retreated back under the carts where the situation was total chaos.

The two gliders wheeled around, planning to try the same trick again. This time the boys didn't come out to meet them. Only Feretti, guessing what the pilots were up to, stepped out from the cart. He waited until the first glider had spent its fire, then aimed the grenade launcher at the second. Bam! A shell struck the engine. The pilot tried to land, but crashed into the side of the pyramid, instead. As the flaming wreckage tumbled all around, the shepherd boys leaped from their hiding place, cheering with all their might.

O'Neil raced toward the bomb, pulling the access card from his pocket. 3:39, 3:38. Where was the code to abort detonation? He looked up to see Anubis in the doorway. The jackal was aiming his laser rifle at him. There was nowhere to hide. In desperation O'Neil lifted the silver tray the bomb had been on, and held it in front of him. The mirrorlike surface bent the laser beam back in the direction it had been fired from. Anubis dropped his weapon and ducked behind the doorway.

O'Neil kicked the weapon out of the way. He had to deal with the bomb first. Then he would take care of Anubis. But he saw that the jackal was back. Now he had huge, gleaming metallic claws growing out of his hands. O'Neil could see that the claws were made of the same material as Anubis's helmet. That qualified them as deadly weapons. O'Neil was just wondering what to do, when he heard the udajeet explode on impact with the pyramid.

"Come," Ra whispered to Daniel, holding the sarcophagus open. "If you come closer, I will not hurt her." Just then, the glider crashed into the pyramid, shaking the walls with a deafening explosion. Ra shrieked and cowered behind the sarcophagus. In all his years as supreme pharaoh and god, his palace had never been attacked, and it terrified him. He looked at Daniel as if begging for sympathy, then turned and fled the room.

Seizing his chance, Daniel bent over the sarcophagus. Sha'uri was breathing! The magic coffin had brought her back to life. But she was still unconscious. Daniel scooped her up in his arms and dashed out into the throne room.

Kawalsky and company were out of ammunition, and the remaining glider pilots knew it. They had swooped down right over the troops' heads, inviting ground fire. When there wasn't any, they had coasted to a landing a short distance away. The glider doors opened, and two Horuses stepped out. They took out their laser rifles and started marching toward the obelisks.

O'Neil began to punch in the abort code. He knew Anubis was striding toward him, but he had no choice. They were almost out of time. Anubis's death claw swung toward him. O'Neil ducked. Shrrrk! The claw cut deeply, but not into the colonel. Instead, it shredded Daniel's book of ancient Egyptian hieroglyphs, which O'Neil had snatched from the tray of captured artifacts, and thrown up as a shield. O'Neil grabbed Anubis's arm and twisted it behind his back. "Bad dog!" he hissed into the beast's ear. "Don't you know it's a crime to mistreat books?"

He yanked the jackal's arm out of its socket. Anubis howled in pain. O'Neil kicked him in the jaw. When he was sure the warrior was unconscious, he dragged the jackal to the medallion. O'Neil pinned him down, half on the medallion and half off.

Daniel laid Sha'uri on top of the medallion. Then he frantically looked around for some way to turn the device on. Ra's child slaves were gathered around watching.

"Help us," he pleaded. The children only stared and laughed nervously. *"Ya'ani!"* A scream echoed through the room and the children took off. Ra strode toward Daniel, his eyes aflame. "The time for games is over," he hissed.

Daniel looked at Ra, then looked down at Sha'uri. Somehow he had to buy enough time to get her to safety. He plowed forward to fight the golden pharaoh stalking toward him.

Ra stretched out his hand, which was fitted with the gold quartz glove. A beam of blue light blazed out of the gem, knocking Daniel to the ground. Daniel struggled to his feet and resumed his advance. This time, Ra caught him with the full paralyzing force of the deadly jewel. Daniel's arms and legs snapped backward in pain, felling him near the edge of the medallion. Then Ra reached across to where his prey knelt stunned and lowered his hand onto Daniel's head. Daniel's face began to ripple like a reflection in a liquid mirror. In a matter of seconds, Daniel would be dead.

O'Neil knew what to do. He bent over and pressed the button on Anubis's wrist device. It was the button he had seen the jackal use to start up the medallion. "Give my regards to King Tut!" O'Neil muttered.

The cold blue laser pierced the air, inches above Anubis's head. The jackal-headed warrior, awake now, began to scream. Bucking as hard as he could, he tried to break free of O'Neil's grasp. But the colonel held on like a pit bull terrier. Remembering how the blue laser had sliced through Sha'uri's robe, he waited to see what it would do when it reached Anubis's neck.

Daniel had seen the laser cut through Sha'uri's robe as well. Now when he saw the blue laser appear above the medallion, the memory of this struggled up through the blinding pain in his head. Daniel grabbed Ra's hand, holding it in place. When the laser got there, the pharaoh-god would lose his arm.

Ra was confused. Why did the man want to keep his hand where it was, keep being tortured? He shrugged. It didn't matter. The prisoner would be dead in a matter of seconds. The blue light kept coming.

Then Ra grew bored with the game. He tried to pull back his hand. "Let go!" Ra commanded. Yet Daniel held on, even though the world was turning black, and he was sure he was about to die. Then something caught his eye: the disk on Ra's neck. It was the medallion Catherine had given him for luck. Daniel reached out and tore the disk from Ra's neck as the laser completed its circle and sealed. The laser froze Ra's arm in place.

As Daniel and Sha'uri were swallowed up in the blue light, so was part of Ra. The blue laser cut a clean line through his forearm. In exchange the machine delivered the severed head of his greatest warrior, Anubis.

Ra shrieked in agony. He had to get to the sarcophagus. The machine would grow back his lost arm. But it wouldn't help him much, if he bled to death here on the floor. He screamed for help. But the throne room was silent. Ra stood up and staggered toward the sarcophagus, all the while promising that he would punish with death those who had ignored his calls for help.

23
00:03, 00:02, 00:01

O'Neil recognized Ra's severed hand right away. Sha'uri and Daniel were both out cold. He turned back to the bomb in a panic. 3:46 and counting down.

Even if Daniel were awake, it would take longer than that to fire up the StarGate. O'Neil had to shut the bomb down. He raced over and punched in the abort code. As he pressed the Enter button, O'Neil breathed a sigh of relief. Then he saw the ticker was still counting down. 3:22, 3:21.

Shocked, O'Neil searched his memory. Why wasn't the code working? What had he forgotten? The bomb just kept ticking.

Kawalsky knew they had no choice. They were out of ammunition, and each moment brought the Horus guards a step closer. "We've got to surrender," he said.

"What!" barked Feretti.

"We'll lose any fight we start. We've got to surrender and hope O'Neil's still alive."

"If he is, he's in Colorado by now."

"It's not us, Feretti. It's the kids. If we surrender they may not kill them. They may just take them prisoner."

Feretti looked at the exhausted shepherd boys and knew Kawalsky was right. "Okay," he said. "Let's do it." The two threw down their empty rifles and marched out from the obelisks. One by one, the shepherd boys followed, their hands in the air. Skaara surrendered last. He alone wanted to fight to the end.

When they neared the guards, the troops fell to their knees, hoping this would save them from an instant death. But in the silence that followed, they heard the Horuses clicking open their weapons and preparing to fire.

Kawalsky rose to his feet. He raced toward Ra's warriors, hoping to take the first shot. Maybe if they killed him, they would spare the children. But then a roaring sound filled his ears. His heart and feet stopped.

It was the sound of drums. Thousands of drums beating at the same time. A thousand men of Nagada stood on the dunes around them, all shouting and beating drums and kettles and pots as hard as they could.

The two Horus soldiers hesitated, not sure what to do. Then they lifted their guns to fire on the soldiers and the shepherd boys. All at once a hundred men rushed

183

down from the dunes to form a human wall between the hawk-heads and their prisoners. Then hundreds more rushed down to surround Ra's soldiers on all remaining sides. The crowd was dancing and laughing and shouting. Like a strong animal held in reins too long, the people of Nagada were surging with energy, ready to explode.

Suddenly, Kasuf appeared at the crest of the dune. He shouted at the crowd to stop. Silence fell.

One of the Horus guards spat out at the crowd, "Ra, Lord of the Sun, repays both praise and disobedience many times over. Praise Ra, Lord of Justice!"

But the crowd had heard enough. Kasuf raised his staff and they spilled down over the sand dunes toward the Horuses. Ra's soldiers squeezed off as many shots as they could, but nothing could stop the people from coming. A battle cry exploded from them as they swept over Ra's hated henchmen like a storming sea.

Ra hurried to the sarcophagus and threw himself on the stone bed inside. Trembling, he pulled the shroud over his head. The lid closed over him. The quiet hum of the machine was as soothing as a lullaby. It meant the pain in his arm would stop, and in time a new arm would grow. Being in the machine meant undisturbed comfort and the peaceful sleep of the dead. The sarcophagus was the closest thing he had to affection. Ra had no friends, no loved ones. Only slaves and the children whom he treated as his pets. Ra had all the material comforts imaginable. But there was no one in his world for him to talk to. Ra closed his eyes, feeling a familiar calm wash over him. Suddenly, voices disturbed his rest.

He forced himself out of the sarcophagus and staggered back to his private chamber. At the window, he watched the crowd below sweep over his soldiers. Soon Ra had seen enough. It was time to escape.

He went to the control panel of his spaceship. Almost instantly, the golden walls of the pyramid whirred to life. As the ship prepared for takeoff, Ra's children rushed toward the golden medallion, eager to escape before Ra kept his promise to punish them.

When the Horus soldiers were taken care of outside, the crowd rushed up the ramp to the pyramid door. Working under Kawalsky's direction, they lifted the door and streamed inside.

Some hesitated, afraid to enter the palace of Ra. But others ran ahead eagerly. Suddenly, a loud clap, like the sound of thunder, silenced them all. It was followed by the deep rumbling of Ra's spaceship jolting into action.

The Almighty Ra was running away.

The people of Nagada had won. The crowd exploded into a wild, joyful cry.

Daniel's whole face was a giant purple bruise. So was most of the rest of him. But he looked worse than he was. He had gotten away from Ra's quartz just in time.

The rumbling of the spaceship engines woke him. He looked around, then smiled. Sha'uri was next to him. She was just waking up, too. They were both alive!

Suddenly, Daniel remembered everything else. He bolted up. Where was O'Neil? Where was the bomb? He saw O'Neil across the room, bending over the steel canisters. Then he saw that the bomb was still ticking. 00:41, 00:40, 00:39.

Daniel rushed over to O'Neil in a panic. "Turn it off! He's leaving! We won!"

"I'm trying. It's been rigged. It won't shut off."

"Rigged? By who?"

"Military intelligence," O'Neil replied grimly.

00:22, 00:21, 00:20.

The two men stared at the bomb, stunned. Then they began talking at the same time. Both of them had just had the same idea. 00:18, 00:17, 00:16.

The crowd was celebrating. People were dancing, jumping on each other, whooping, hollering, hugging, even tackling each other. Only one person in the crowd was not enjoying the victory, and that was Skaara. The boy knew they'd won, and knew it had all been worth it, but he'd lost his friend Nabeh.

At last, Skaara spotted Nabeh's helmet still lying in the middle of the ramp. He decided to get it in memory of his buddy. He pushed through the crowd. But before he could reach the helmet another man seized it.

The man didn't get two feet before a scorched, bloody

hand reached out from the rubble and locked on to the helmet. It was Nabeh! Skaara leaped over to him and squeezed him in his arms.

"Did you see me, Skaara? I was flying."

Skaara smiled through tears. "I saw you Nabeh."

The other shepherd boys, and Kawalsky and Feretti, came rushing over. Kawalsky checked Nabeh's injuries. He had gotten two dozen cuts at least. Feretti looked at Kawalsky anxiously.

"Its not as bad as it looks. He's going to be okay."

Skaara and Nabeh didn't understand. Kawalsky put his hand on Nabeh's shoulder. "You're going to be fine," he said slowly. "You're a tough little guy."

Ra's children came racing from all directions. The older ones helping the younger ones, they leaped onto the medallion. At the push of a button, the blue light began rising from the metal floor. Ra stared at them, his amber eyes wide.

"You cannot leave me!" he screamed.

It was partly a command, and partly a plea. But it was too late. The blue light completed its circle, and the children were swallowed up in a rush of light.

In their place, O'Neil's bomb materialized. It was the last thing Ra would ever see. The countdown numbers flashed, sending Ra news of his own destruction. 00:09, 00:08, 00:07.

When Ra realized who had sent this unwelcome gift, a howl tore out of him like a gust of poison wind.

Just as he had taken over the boy Ra's body ten thousand years ago, now he tried to leave it. The alien escaped the human flesh, but could not escape the spaceship. 00:02, 00:01. In a flash it was over.

Daniel, Sha'uri, and O'Neil staggered out of the pyramid just in time to watch Ra's spaceship disappear from view.

"He's gone!" Daniel announced.

The ship was already thousands of miles away when the timer on the bomb flashed to zero. Great white arcs of light filled the sky, giving the people on the ground the best firework show they would ever see.

"And he's not coming back," O'Neil added.

Another roar rose from the crowd.

Now Ra's slave children came running out of the pyramid. They looked in fear at the people of Nagada, but the miners and their families welcomed them with open arms.

Kasuf stood up to thank the visitors. But Skaara ran past him up the ramp. Facing O'Neil and the other earthlings, Skaara lifted his hand in a pretty decent military salute. The other shepherd boys did the same. Kawalsky and Feretti ate it up. They loved these kids for all they had done. They joined the boys in saluting the colonel.

O'Neil choked up. He knew it was silly, but it got to him. Slowly, he lifted his hand and returned Skaara's salute.

Now Sha'uri raised Daniel's hand high in the air. The crowd cheered the man they had once feared as a god, but now respected as a friend. Daniel leaned over and kissed Sha'uri. For the first time in his life, he felt he truly belonged.

The crowd hoisted the couple onto their shoulders, and carried them out into the desert. Suddenly, Daniel spotted Little Bit. The mastadge was on top of a dune, waiting for his turn to congratulate the hero of the day. Sha'uri saw Daniel frown at the mangiest beast on either planet. She whispered something to the men carrying him. Laughing and cheering, they ran Daniel straight toward the bad breath and slimy tongue of the affectionate mongrel. Daniel shot a look at Sha'uri, a look that said the same thing in any language. "I'll get you for this!"

24
IT BROUGHT ME LUCK

Daniel held a flare in one hand, his notebook in the other. Under his directions, Kawalsky turned the inner ring of the StarGate, sliding the constellations into place. As the final symbol was wheeled into place with a click, the strange machine came alive. Then Daniel and Kawalsky raced back to the medallion room to join the others.

The medallion room and the great hall beyond it were filled with people who had come to watch the event. Even though they'd seen it before, Daniel and the soldiers were peeking up at the StarGate like a bunch of boys who'd snuck into the movies. The show was fantastic.

The light came pouring out of ring's seven golden clamps like ropes of water, rising up against gravity.

They slowly filled the ring's center, becoming a shimmering white surface of a bubbling pool.

But this time it wasn't the ring's light show that was the star of the show. It was the music. The soldiers had heard it before in the silo, but there with all computers pulsing they hadn't really heard it. This time, in torchlight, in the temple-like atmosphere of the ancient pyramid, the music was overwhelmingly awesome.

As the song rose to its climax, the pool of light began to slosh over the rim of the StarGate. A second later, the liquid light exploded into the room like the grasping hand of a god. Everyone in the great hall gasped at the terrifying power of the mysterious machine. But when they took their hands away from their eyes, the energy had already been sucked back through the ring, and was tearing across the universe.

The soldiers stood up. It was time to go. Skaara approached O'Neil. The colonel took his hand and shook it. Unlike the first time, Skaara did not run away screaming. He shook O'Neil's hand back. In fact, O'Neil was sure the boy would never run away from anything again, and neither would he.

The four Marines started up the stairs that led to the gate. Daniel watched from below. "Hey," Feretti called to him. "I want you to know, I always knew you'd get us back." He winked.

"Yeah, right," said Kawalsky. He turned to Daniel. "Thanks," he said simply. Daniel slapped him on the back and turned to face O'Neil.

"You going to be okay?" O'Neil asked, even though he knew the answer.

Daniel turned to Sha'uri and smiled. "Yeah. And you?"

O'Neil knew what Daniel meant. Daniel had been right when he said in the cave that O'Neil was in a hurry to die. But not now, not today. Today he was thinking about getting back to his wife, Sarah. He was ready to try. To try and live again.

"Yeah, I'll be okay." Daniel knew it was the truth. O'Neil would be okay. "Anyhow, this place suits you, Jackson. You'll probably be down in the catacombs for the next six months."

"You'll come and visit, won't you?" Even as the words left his lips, Daniel felt funny about them. Several million light years was a long way from home.

"It won't be up to me," answered O'Neil. "That'll be up to my superiors."

"Military intelligence?" Daniel asked.

O'Neil smiled. "Yeah, military intelligence."

The men stood silent for a moment.

"Do me a favor." Daniel handed over Catherine's medallion. "Tell Catherine it brought me luck."

"You bet." Swallowing his emotions, O'Neil turned and walked into the StarGate's beam.

The others followed him; their images froze in midstep before they vanished in a blur of light.

Daniel watched long after the soldiers had disappeared, until the ring spun itself around and shut down, and the bowels of the pyramid returned to the darkness of torchlight. At last, he turned to lead Skaara and Sha'uri and the other Nagadans out of the darkness of the pyramid into the desert, where the last of the three suns was setting.

As they began the long walk back to the city, Little Bit wandered to the top of the dune. Standing over the Nagadans, she threw back her head and sounded a beautiful farewell cry.

THE PAGEMASTER

A novelization by Todd Strasser

Imagine meeting Long John Silver, Dr Jekyll and Moby Dick – in one day!

Richard Tyler is the world's most cautious kid. Fearful of accidents wherever he turns, Richard's greatest fear becomes reality when he gets caught in a freak thunderstorm. He crashes his bike (with extra-special safety features) and rushes for cover into his local library.

There he meets the mysterious Pagemaster, who takes him into a fantasy world where books literally come to life. It's not a journey for the faint-hearted, but through it Richard develops a new confidence in himself and the world around him.

Based on the film *The Pagemaster* starring Macaulay Culkin and Christopher Lloyd.

FRANKENSTEIN

Mary Shelley
Adapted by Robin Waterfield

Life has many mysteries, but there is none greater than the secret of creation. Victor Frankenstein the brilliant scientist believes he has discovered that secret and creates a life form to prove his theory. The dire and hideous consequences of this he could never have imagined, as Frankenstein's dream of life into a nightmare of death.

This chillingly terrifying tale is famous as one of the world's greatest horor stories. It has been retold many times in book and on film. This version is a faithful adaptation of the original Mary Shelley novel.

THE NIGHTMARE BEFORE CHRISTMAS
Daphne Skinner

Under the orange disc of the moon in Hallowe'en Land the creatures of the night are busy. Jack Skellington is the king of this strange world, but lately he's grown tired of the same old frights. Then by chance he discovers Christmas Town. What a wonderful place, he thinks, and what a wonderful idea if Hallowe'en Land came to visit Christmas Town.

Scary, funny and touching, this is the novel based on the film *The Nightmare Before Christmas*.

SONIC THE HEDGEHOG ADVENTURE
GAMEBOOK 4
THE ZONE ZAPPER
Nigel Gross and Jon Sutherland

It's not unusual for Robotnik to go round messing up the Green Hill Zone. This time, however, he's built a brand-new machine which turns everything good into bad – even Tails! Sonic faces the fight of his life with his best friends. Will they survive and will he?

Think fast and act quickly – Sonic's going to need all the help he can get!